P. M. Hubbard and The Murder Room

>>> This title is part of The Murder Room, our series dedicated to making available out-of-print or hard-to-find titles by classic crime writers.

Crime fiction has always held up a mirror to society. The Victorians were fascinated by sensational murder and the emerging science of detection; now we are obsessed with the forensic detail of violent death. And no other genre has so captivated and enthralled readers.

Vast troves of classic crime writing have for a long time been unavailable to all but the most dedicated frequenters of second-hand bookshops. The advent of digital publishing means that we are now able to bring you the backlists of a huge range of titles by classic and contemporary crime writers, some of which have been out of print for decades.

From the genteel amateur private eyes of the Golden Age and the femmes fatales of pulp fiction, to the morally ambiguous hard-boiled detectives of mid twentieth-century America and their descendants who walk our twenty-first century streets, The Murder Room has it all. >>>

The Murder Room
Where Criminal Minds Meet

themurderroom.com

P. M. Hubbard (1910–1980)

Praised by critics for his clean prose style, characterization, and the strong sense of place in his novels, Philip Maitland Hubbard was born in Reading, in Berkshire and brought up in Guernsey, in the Channel Islands. He was educated at Oxford, where he won the Newdigate Prize for English verse in 1933. From 1934 until its disbandment in 1947 he served with the Indian Civil Service. On his return to England he worked for the British Council, eventually retiring to work as a freelance writer. He contributed to a number of publications, including *Punch*, and wrote 16 novels for adults as well as two children's books. He lived in Dorset and Scotland, and many of his novels draw on his interest in and knowledge of rural pursuits and folk religion.

Kill Claudio

P. M. Hubbard

An Orion book

Copyright © Caroline Dumonteil, Owain Rhys Phillips and Maria
Marcela Appleby Gomez 1979, 2013

The right of P. M. Hubbard to be identified as the author of this work
has been asserted in accordance with the Copyright, Designs and Patents
Act 1988.

This edition published by
The Orion Publishing Group Ltd
Orion House
5 Upper St Martin's Lane
London WC2H 9EA

An Hachette UK company
A CIP catalogue record for this book is available from the British Library

ISBN 978 1 4719 0075 4

www.orionbooks.co.uk

CHAPTER 1.

I did not mean to kill the rabbit, but it ran suddenly across the track at a nice distance, and my gun came up without any conscious decision on my part. The rabbit vanished into the rough, but I knew I had hit it, and it could not be far off, so I went to look for it. I never found it, because I found the man instead, and that put the rabbit out of my head. If I had not shot the rabbit and gone to look for it, I should never have found the man, and neither would anyone else, or not until the scavengers had removed any great hope of identification, and probably not even then. Not many people go that way. The heather would have grown up through the picked bones, and the bones would have gone neatly down into the peat along with all the other riff-raff of the centuries. But I had to go and shoot the rabbit, and had now found the man, and here I was, stuck with him. He was no possible concern of mine, but to report him was the civilised thing to do, and there was even the possibility that not to report him might land me in trouble. So I took a fairly good look at him (there was still no reason not to), and then walked back to get in touch with the police. But I walked at my own pace, and was conscious of no special excitement, let alone of any concern. I remember there was one moment when I checked in my stride, because something I had seen in the man's face made me wonder a bit, but I could not put my finger on it, and just went on walking.

1

I made my report and put the police on their way, and left them to it. I had nothing to tell them that they could not see for themselves. Later, quite a lot later, a fairly senior policeman and inspector, or somesuch, came and took my statement, but that was the merest formality. When it was finished, he put his things away and sat back in his chair. He crossed one leg over the other, which made him look a lot less formal, and sat there looking at me. Then he turned his head sideways, as if merely to be looking at me like that was an intrusion, and said, "You'll pardon my asking, sir, but you don't know of anyone who might wish you ill for any reason?"

It was so much a standard line of dialogue that he seemed to find it embarrassing, and I was sure that the curiously stately "wish you ill" was the deliberate avoidance of a cliché. All the same, it jolted me fairly out of my mood of determined detachment. I leant forward, as if to cancel out the effect of his sitting back, and said, "Good God, you don't mean—?" Then the obvious illogicality of what I had been going to say stopped me in my stride, and my question hung there until he came in again.

This time he took refuge in cliché as clearly as he had avoided it before. He said, "We are treating the case as one of murder, yes, sir."

I nodded and then frowned at him. The frown was meant to express honest bewilderment, but I was suddenly conscious of my heart beating. I said, "But you asked—I mean, it was him that got murdered, not me. I don't know who he was, but—"

He did not wait for me to make the obvious point. He said, "That is so, sir, yes. And we know who he was, and we don't know why anyone should want to kill him. But it seems he was killed yesterday evening, possibly in the dusk,

2

and he was certainly killed from behind, and not far from your cottage. And you wouldn't have noticed it, but he was dressed very much as you are and was about your size and build. So it did occur to us to wonder whether he might have been killed in mistake for you. And about you, sir, of course, we know next to nothing, only that you come from the south and have taken Mr. Morton's cottage for a bit, and made the booking through his agents in Brancastle. So it seemed worth asking."

He was so apologetic about it that he almost disarmed me, but not quite. So far as the unknown up in the heather was concerned, there was nothing on my conscience, and so far as I could see nothing to get me involved beyond the mere fact of my finding him. But I was damned if I was going to discuss my past with the inspector, and saw no good reason why I should. I smiled at him, and this time the smile came with a more practised assurance. I shook my head at him almost gaily. "I don't expect I'm more universally loved than anyone else," I said, "but I can't really believe anyone would bother to follow me all the way up here to do me in. Apart from the fact that on one knows I'm here, I mean except the agents and presumably Mr. Morton." I thought for a moment. "Incidentally," I said, "do we know what the murdered man was doing here, whoever he was? I mean, was he a local? I've certainly never seen him around. But then I haven't been here long."

My assurance seemed to take a weight off his mind, though that did not make much sense either because he must have been badly in need of some explanation. At any rate, he shook his head almost as cheerfully as I had. "Not a local man," he said. "Or not what you'd call local. He came from Brancastle. A Mr. Mowbray. We got on to him pretty quickly, in fact. There was a tailor's tag in his jacket pocket

3

which somebody seems to have overlooked. They're not so common as they were, of course. What I mean is, there wasn't anything else on him at all to show who he was, and most of us carry something, even if it's only an old envelope, but here there was nothing but the tag, which looks as if someone went over him, but not quite thoroughly enough. But what he was doing here we can't say. Unless he was brought, of course."

I looked at him with friendly interest, and listened to him with only half my mind. I was picking over my memory for Mowbrays, and could not come up with a single one. And yet I felt I ought to be able to. I would not have had the inspector think so for the world, but I had a feeling I ought to know this Mr. Mowbray, who had come here from Brancastle only a few days after I had. But even with only half my mind working on it, the lack of Mowbrays in my past seemed singularly complete.

I smiled a sort of respectful smile, partly for the dead man's sake and partly for the inspector's, and said, "Well, I'm sorry I can't be of more use, and I'm sorry for the chap, whoever he was. Any family?"

"A wife," he said. "No children." I nodded with a proper relief, and he got up to go. He said, "I don't know what you have in mind." He was all hesitation again. "I mean," he said, "I don't know if you'll feel like staying on here after this has happened?"

I was not going to tell him what I felt like, but clearly there was only one thing I could say, and I said it, looking at him with a sort of mildly indignant surprise. "Oh, but—of course," I said. "I mean, I can see no reason to change my plans, as long as you don't mind my being here. I was only going to be here a fortnight anyway. Will that be all right for you?"

For the first time he did not wholly disguise the speculation in the way he looked at me. "That's up to you, sir," he said. "But you'll be reasonably careful, if you don't mind. I'd rather you locked your doors at night and didn't go out walking in the dusk, as Mr. Mowbray seems to have done. We've no reason to think you're at any risk whatever, but we don't know much yet, and that's the truth, and we don't want a second murder on our hands, and I assume you don't either —especially not yours. So, as I say, be a bit careful, and let us know you're around. I won't ask you to report formally every day, but if you can, make sure somebody sees you, or we'll be having to send a man up to look for you, and frankly we're going to have enough on our hands without that."

I promised him all he asked, and he took himself off. I shut the door and went back to my chair, and it was only then I really started to wonder. I wondered what the inspector was really thinking. I wondered if I had done and said the right things. In particular, I wondered if I had been right not to ask for more details of the murder. I wanted to know them rather badly, but they would be published, and I could wait. The only thing was whether my not showing more curiosity had struck the inspector as odd, especially when I had found the body in the first place. But it was too late to worry about that now.

In the meantime, I assumed what I had, without examining the assumption, assumed from the start. By now, after all, I knew that the man had been killed—and killed from behind. I did not think there had been any shooting, and I had seen enough for myself to exclude blunt instruments or any form of strangulation. There was nothing to exclude my original immediate assumption of the small, almost bloodless puncture between the ribs, and the upward-sloping incision just deep enough to reach the heart. The fact remained that

5

I had assumed it from the start, and the next thing I wondered about was why.

I had seen enough of it at one time, heaven knows, but it was a long time ago now. It was years since I had even seen one of those long steel blades, let alone handled one. As for the people, they were further back still, a list of names printed on a white ground, because that was the only way I remembered names (there had certainly been no such lists at the time), or a row of faces, bunched or in line, familiar faces, but each with its own familiar inscrutability. The faces in the line had come and gone over a period of time, and those that went never came back, so that when I recalled them, as I did sometimes, even now, I never got the same bunch of faces twice, nor could I really be sure that any particular bunch of faces had ever co-existed, as a bunch, in my actual experience. The visual memory, I find, is a powerful and accurate instrument, but it takes little count of time. I have known middle-aged men whose visual image in my mind has never succeeded in superseding their remembered appearance at fourteen or fifteen, and this is bound to make for confusion.

Meanwhile, I had found a dead man lying on his back in the heather with nothing but a mild surprise showing on his face. For all appearances, he could perfectly well have died of heart failure, but I had assumed as the manner of his death a particular way of killing which I had hardly thought of in the last twenty years, and as I say, I wondered why. That was why my mind had gone to work so eagerly on the name Mowbray when the inspector had mentioned it, but there was no Mowbray on my imagined lists, and never had been. I gave it up, and went about my business in the cottage.

It was quite late in the evening when I remembered that

moment on my way down the hill, when I had checked in my stride because something in the dead face had worried me. When I did remember it, I sat down to think it over. I wondered if my memory had been up to its tricks again, trying subconsciously to make a connection between the new dead face and a face I had once known living, but failing to convince my conscious mind. I tried, inevitably, but inevitably with no success, comparing the dead face with my bunches of remembered faces, conducting a sort of supernal identification parade in my head and trying to establish a doubtful identity across what Prospero calls the dark backward and abysm of time. But I knew from experience that this was no job for the conscious mind, and that wrestling with it might do more harm than good, and after a bit I gave it up and put the thing out of my head.

More practically, I wondered what the inspector was doing about me, and how far he would push his enquiries. For all his kindly concern, I did not for a moment suppose that he had excluded the possibility that I might have killed the man myself, and the fact that I had not would not, as I knew very well, necessarily prevent complications which I was in general anxious to avoid. To the best of my belief, I had nothing to fear from the law, but that did not mean that I was anxious to tangle with it.

I did not go walking in the dusk, and I did lock my doors and windows before I went to bed. I even shifted my bed from where I had found it when I came to a corner not directly covered from any of the windows, and put the gun, loaded, beside it. Needless to say, I was not doing all this to please the inspector. I did it as a matter of ingrained routine, because wherever the truth lay I found myself, in my mind, back on what might be called a war footing, and I simply acted accordingly. I did not seriously expect to be attacked.

Other things apart, if the inspector was right, and the man Mowbray had been killed in mistake for me, I did not think that the case had had enough publicity yet for the killer to realise what he had done. I took my precautions as easily as you slip into a particular set of old clothes when there is a particular dirty job to be done. Having taken them, I went to bed and slept quite peacefully.

I do not know what time of the night it was, but it was still pitch dark, when I woke up and rolled over on to my back and opened my eyes and said, "Mowbray be damned. That's Peter Gaston." I said it out loud in the utter stillness, which was foolish of me, or at least inconsistent with my earlier precautions. Anyone might have been listening, and I should have been in much worse difficulties if there had been someone. The important point, of course, was not that the dead man was Peter Gaston, but that I knew he was. In fact, no one was listening, and I started out with the advantage which my undisclosed knowledge gave me.

That apart, I knew several other things once I had the name. I knew that Peter had come up here because I had. Anything else would be too wild a coincidence to be acceptable. I did not know why he had come up, or what he was intending to do, but he had been up here because I was. Knowing Peter, I had no doubt that so far as I was concerned his intentions had been friendly. I also knew he had been killed because he had come up here. It was still possible that he had been killed by mistake, but he would not have been killed at all if he had stayed on quietly in Brancastle as Mr. Mowbray, whom nobody had any reason to harm. But what Peter had wanted with me, and what somebody else had wanted with Peter or me or both of us—of that I had no idea at all.

I knew, well enough, when I had last seen him, but I had

not known him very long. I had not known him in the Army (we had all started in the Army, Commandos mostly), and I do not think he was very long with the Establishment. We called it the Establishment more in self-derision than in derision. I never remember more than one or two of us at any time who took ourselves seriously. So far as I know, it never had a name of its own. It merely existed and functioned as a series of personal contacts and cash transactions. In recent years there has been all this talk of mercenaries, but that is nonsense. It is a mercenary age, and whatever it is we do, all but a tiny minority of us are in it for the money. Beside that, as I see it, what you actually do for the money is of minor importance. We certainly never did anything against the law in our own country. We did not even work in our own country, or not as far as I ever heard. If we had, it would probably have been illegal, but what we did elsewhere was for the local authorities to judge, and it was very seldom the local law that caught up with us.

I had been on several jobs with Peter during his time with the Establishment, including my last. We had agreed about a lot of things, and one of the things we had agreed about was leaving the Establishment, but, in fact, I had left before he had. I never to my knowledge saw him again, but if for any reason he had wanted to keep tabs on me, he would have had no special difficulty in doing it. As I say, we were not really undercover men. We merely signed off and got ourselves, if we were lucky, more ordinary jobs. I had not even changed my name, as he for some reason had. If there had been something Peter had known about and I had not, and which he had later decided to bring me in on, there was nothing to stop him getting in touch with me. I wished I knew what it was he had tried to tell me about, only when he had tried, someone had stopped him once and for all, and now I could never ask him. If I wanted to know, there was nothing for it but to find out for myself, and I thought there were several good reasons why I should. For one thing, the business might be, and probably was, something of importance to me. For another, if Peter had been killed in mistake for me, I clearly could not safely leave things as they were. Next time they might get it right. And lastly, someone had, in whatever circumstances, killed Peter. I am not unduly swayed by sentiment, but I resented that.

CHAPTER 2.

I was called to give evidence at the inquest. I suppose that was inevitable, though, in fact, they might just as well have started with the police. I answered all their questions truthfully, except that when the coroner asked me if I had ever seen the deceased before, I said I had not. I was not at all sure what business it was of his anyway, and I had my own safety to think of, but I was glad the question had been asked. What I was mainly interested in was the other people in court, but I saw no one at all likely. The only remote possibility turned out on enquiry to be the crime reporter of the local paper. That on the whole did not surprise me. Even if the opposition had not meant to kill Peter, they would know by now that they had, and that I was still alive. The only thing that concerned them was whether I had recognised him, and they could get my answer to that without hearing my evidence in person. The widow—Mrs. Mowbray, presumably—was not called. There was formal evidence of identity from someone Peter had worked with. The whole thing amounted to nothing at all. The jury returned the inevitable verdict against a person or persons unknown, and the police said investigations were proceeding.

Nobody called me to Peter's funeral, but I went all the same. I went because I wanted to have a look at Peter's widow. This was an occasion she could not miss, and, once there, she was bound to be a central figure, open to observation from among the spectators. If I knew anything about places like Brancastle, there would be plenty of those. I wanted to observe her because I had it in mind to ask her some questions, and before I took that rather dangerous step, I must have some idea what sort of a person she was. With a man it is difficult to make a judgement of that sort without speaking to him, but women are different. As with animals, I find that you learn more about them the less they know you are watching them.

It was a sad occasion, not only because I had liked Peter and was upset by his death. It was sad because, as funerals go, it was so obviously getting the worst of both worlds. You can have a very small, completely private funeral, with only a handful of interested people there, or you can have a big funeral where the number of people there is in itself a sign of sympathy and admiration. Either is all right, but this was neither. From what I could see, there were only two mourners, the widow and another, older, woman whom I took to be a mother or an older sister, but there was no privacy at all. There were people everywhere, but they were spectators, not participants. I did not try to get a close view of Peter's widow. I did not want to get into the centre of the picture myself, and it was not her face I was interested in, it was her whole style and way of going about the thing.

I thought that was admirable. To a woman who wanted to, it would have been a marvellous occasion for playing the tragic widow, but there was nothing of that about her at all, not even in her dress. She seemed to know exactly what she was doing, and to be perfectly serious about it, but so far as other people were concerned, apart from her one companion, she might have been alone. I did see one or two people try to speak to her, but from what I could see, she simply looked through them. I wondered whether she had even

12

heard them, she was so self-absorbed in the business of bury-
ing her husband. I was not prepared, at my age and with my
experience, to commit myself to the admiration of anyone,
more especially a woman, but I had to admit that there, in
the vulgarity of the municipal cemetery and among all those
intrusive people, I was much struck by Peter's widow.

Whether the impression she had made on me was an argument for or against what I had in mind I was not at all sure.
I saw her at once, not merely as a source of information, but
as a person to be reckoned with, and that cut both ways. I
went back to the cottage in two minds about her, but the
thing was settled for me because the next morning I had a
letter from her by post.

The writing confirmed my impression of her, straightforward, determined, completely without frills. She simply
asked me to come and see her that evening, giving a time,
which would be well after dark, but adding no explanation
whatever. I parked the car some way away and walked to
the house. By then there was nothing but the sort of lighting
you get in residential side-streets, and the windows of the
house itself were closely curtained, but from what I could
see, it was all ordinary to the point of being nondescript. It
was a four-room detached bungalow with a garage at the
side, plenty big enough for a couple without children provided they shared a bedroom. It told me nothing about what
Peter had been up to all these years. It suggested financial
competence and social respectability, but no pretensions.
This did not necessarily mean that he was not in the money.
Even in these status-ridden days, not everyone who makes a
bit goes in for patios and swimming-pools, and I could not
see Peter doing so, nor indeed, from what I had seen of her,
Peter's wife. The fact remained that he had had his clothes

13

made by a bespoke tailor, and that, as the inspector had said, is less common that it was.

I walked up the path and rang the bell, and only then there was a first touch of the not entirely usual. A porch-light went on over my head, and I could see the minute glass eye in the door through which I was being, or could be, scrutinised before the door was opened. But even that means little enough now, and the scrutiny, if there was one, was very short. The door opened almost at once, and there she was, looking at me. I stood there and let her look, noticing only that she had one hand still on a very solid-looking latch-lock. She was smaller than I had thought, with a pale face and dark hair, but the whole effect, from the look on her face to the way she stood, was curiously intense. I thought that, if I had had my doubts about the meeting, so by God had she. She said, "Mr. Selby?" and I said "Yes," and she opened the door wider and stood back.

"Come in," she said, and now there was a faintly puzzled expression on her face as she looked at me. Then it cleared. "You were at the funeral," she said, and I thought so much for my being the unobserved observer. She shut the door behind me, and I heard the latch-lock click home. Then she turned and looked at me again and said, "Why?"

I knew enough already to know that I must play it straight or not at all. I said, "I wanted to see you," and for the first time she smiled. I liked her smile, but it was not one to presume on. She smiled to please herself, not me. "That makes two of us," she said. "Well, come in." She opened a door off the narrow hall and showed me into a sitting-room at the front of the house. I did not have time to take in much detail, except that there were a lot of books. But then I had always known Peter for an educated man, and that not only by the standards of the Establishment, where education of

14

any sort was a rarity. She pointed out a chair to me and sat down opposite me. "Why should you want to see me?" she said.

"I wondered what sort of a person Peter had married," I said. "I've known him before, you know. I knew him as Peter Gaston."

I expected some surprise, but she brushed this aside. "I know that," she said. "Peter told me. And why else should you have come to these parts?"

Now I was going to surprise her, but I had to make her understand. "I didn't come to see Peter," I said. "I didn't know he was here. I didn't even recognise him at first. It was only later I remembered who he was. Then I thought he must have been up there to see me—where he was killed, I mean. But I hadn't seen him before that. I still don't know how he even knew I was there."

This time I did surprise her. She leant forward, staring at me. I noticed suddenly how intensely dark her eyes were in her pale face, and wondered for the first time whether she was English. Peter, after all, had not been, or not properly speaking. I did not see Gaston as a native English name. Her English was perfect, but curiously undifferentiated, without any touch of regional or class accent, and that is rare in a native speaker. Meanwhile, she continued to stare at me. She was not quite sure whether she could believe me. Finally she said, "Why did you come?" I had never known a woman waste fewer syllables.

"Pure chance," I said. I found myself clipping my speech to the measure of hers. She was not a person to be overcome with words. "I'm on holiday. I like wild places, especially off-season. I got the cottage through an agency."

She nodded. "I know," she said. "Peter worked there."

I gave it up. "I'm sorry," I said. "Pure coincidence.

Double coincidence. It can happen. I haven't known where Peter was for years. Or even that he had changed his name. I can't make you believe it, but that's the fact."

She had taken her eyes from mine and was staring at the carpet. You do not often see a face as deadpan as that on a woman. Finally she said, "I'm not sure it matters." I waited. There was nothing for me to say, and I could not tell how her mind was working. Then she said, "The fact remains you did come, and Peter knew you had. So, clearly, did someone else. And he'd have assumed you came to see Peter, whether you did or not."

I said, "You're sure it was Peter they meant to kill? The police thought—" but she cut me off.

"It was you," she said. "It must have been. They wouldn't want Peter killed. What they didn't want was you and Peter meeting. It was that they had to prevent. Only they got it wrong." She thought again for a moment. Then she said, "Why did you want to see me?"

"Once I remembered who Peter was," I said, "I assumed then that he must have known I was there, and had come up to see me. Anything else would have been too much of a coincidence. Once I assumed that, I assumed that that was why he was killed. That, and the way he was killed. That meant that it might have been me they were after. In any case, I obviously had to know more, and I wondered whether you could help me. But, in fact, I hadn't made up my mind to come when I got your letter." I paused, looking at her very straight, staring into those rather impenetrable eyes. "Incidentally," I said, "the police still think I might have killed him. Do you?"

She did not hesitate at all. She shook her head decisively. "It doesn't make sense," she said. "Anyway, Peter liked you, and he was never wrong about people."

I gave her a slight smile, and for a moment she smiled back. We were neither of us happy, but the tension had eased between us. "I'm glad of that," I said. "I liked Peter too." She nodded but did not say anything. "That being the case," I said, "do you think you could tell me all you can—anything that seems to have any bearing on what's happened? Even if it means going back a bit. You must remember I've known nothing of Peter for years, not since we last worked together."

"The Establishment?" she said.

"You know about the Establishment?"

She shrugged, and that was definitely not an English gesture. "Only what Peter chose to tell me," she said. She thought for quite a long time after that, staring at the carpet with that expressionless concentration. I looked round the room, waiting for her to make up her mind. It was a nice room. I thought it had been a nice home, unexciting perhaps, but nice, and now Peter was dead, and it was not even a home any more.

She raised her eyes quite slowly without moving her head, and for what seemed a very long moment she looked at me from under almost knitted brows. There was no hostility in the look, but still a lot of speculation. Then she came, almost visibly, to a decision, letting her breath go in a small sigh and raising her head to look straight at me. "All right," she said. "I can help you, perhaps in more ways than you think. And you can help me. If what Peter said about you was right, you're the only person I know who can." She suddenly stopped being businesslike and looked at me with straight appeal. She was a very appealing person when she wanted to be. All the same, I ought to have been warned. "Will you help me," she said, "if I help you?"

Whatever my reasons were, I did not hesitate. "Yes," I

said, "I'll help you in any way I can. I owe that to Peter. It
was my doing he got killed. I didn't intend it, but it happened."

She nodded, and for a moment something like the shadow
of a smile just touched the corners of her mouth. "I think
you do owe it to Peter," she said. She relaxed suddenly and
sat back in her chair, and I found myself doing the same.
She had a trick of dictating the tone of a conversation, so
that I felt compelled, at least outwardly, to fall in with her
changes of mood and even her manner of speaking. Only in
the back of my mind I did not feel relaxed. She said, "What
sort of a person was Peter when you knew him? I didn't
meet him till some time after that."

I thought about that. "Very intelligent," I said. "Very calculating, but always to the extreme limits of risk. Very
charming, very dangerous. I think he was the most perfect
fighting animal I've ever met, and I've met some. In wartime
he'd have made a superb soldier. In peacetime he could
equally have been a top-class criminal. I don't see him working in an estate-agency."

"That was my doing," she said. "He was in with some
very bad people when I met him. I think I pulled him out
just in time. I suppose you can say I tamed him, your fighting animal. Was I wrong? I really think he was happy most
of the time. The job—that was nothing, of course, just something to do. He already had all the money we needed. I
know he"—she hesitated, looking for the words she needed—
"he pulled at the chain at times, but I never let him go. And
now he's dead just the same. It doesn't seem fair."

It did not seem fair to me either, but there was no point in
saying so. I just nodded and waited for her to go on. She
said, "Peter knew something, something from his Establishment days. He never told me what it was, but it was some-

18

thing valuable, something that could mean a lot of money. Only he didn't know enough. I mean, he couldn't do whatever it was or get whatever it was by himself. There were two people who could supply the missing bit, both people he had worked with at the Establishment. One was you. He told me your name. He told me a good deal about you, in fact. Only he said you wouldn't know about the thing unless he told you. Do you see what I mean? You had this missing bit of information, but wouldn't know what it meant unless he told you his bit. The other person who had it did know. I mean, he had the information, and also he knew what it meant, but he couldn't use it without Peter's bit, and he knew Peter wouldn't give him that. Peter never told me his name, but he said he was a man he wouldn't work with at any price. He didn't trust him a yard. It was you he wanted. When the mood took him, he wanted very badly to find you and go after whatever it was with you. That was when he pulled at the chain. It wasn't the money, not really. It was the thing itself, just the feeling that it was there. Can you understand that?"

I nodded. "Knowing Peter," I said, "I can understand it very well.

"Well, there you are, then. That's been the position for years. I didn't understand it all at once, of course. I came to understand a bit more each time the thing came up, but I always managed to talk him out of it. I didn't want the money. I wanted Peter. And then after all these years you had to turn up here, and he had to know about it. He told me, to do him justice. He would. But he told me he had to talk to you, and this time I couldn't stop him. I still hoped nothing might come of it. I suppose I thought you might decide against it between you. Only it never got that far, did it?"

P. M. HUBBARD

I shook my head. It is no good apologising to a woman for her husband's death. "But look," I said, "the thing's finished, isn't it? I don't see how I can help you. Whatever Peter knew, it presumably died with him, and without it I can't even start."

She was looking at me now with an almost fearful intensity. "It didn't," she said. "He left a letter for you, in case he died without seeing you again. I've only now seen it. I never knew it existed. It doesn't mean much to me, but I expect it will to you. I imagine it's all there, if you're prepared to use it."

"And you want me to use it?"

"I want you to use it, yes. It's not the money I want. You can have all that if you can get it."

For a moment or two I stared back into those fierce dark eyes. "Then what do you want?" I said.

"This man," she said. "The man who killed Peter. I want him killed."

20

CHAPTER 3.

There is that tremendous moment in *Much Ado* when Beatrice and Benedick, hitherto united in their resolve to take nothing seriously, not even each other, suddenly find themselves up against something they cannot laugh at. His best friend has casually and totally ruined her best friend, and they are not to know that the thing will be sorted out by Dogberry and his Dad's Army of watchmen, because only Shakespeare could have thought of a thing like that. The first result is to make them admit that they love each other. Then, when Benedick, with a return of his habitual panache, asks what he can do to prove his love, Beatrice drops two words into the silence of the now deserted chapel. "Kill Claudio," she says, and Benedick, shaken and protesting, knows there is no escape.

My position was different from Benedick's in several respects. The man I had been told to kill, although I did not know who he was, was certainly far from being my best friend, if only because of what he had done to Peter and had apparently meant to do to me; and I was not, at least at that stage, in any degree in love with the woman who had told me to kill him. But I was shaken and I saw no probable escape. I was shaken because I did not want to get involved in any more violence, still less to tangle with the criminal law of my own country. I had had too much of the one and hitherto avoided the other, and wanted no change in either re-

21

spect. I nevertheless saw myself trapped for a mixture of reasons, I suppose mostly the same reasons as had made me give my promise in the first place. If Peter had said there was a lot of money in it, the money would be there. I needed money, preferably a lot of money, very badly indeed, and I knew I could not get it except for the stipulated considera- tion. That was because Peter's widow would have to trust me in that respect, and was apparently ready to. I have never found it profitable to examine my moral principles, if that is what they are, but I knew that to collect the money and go off to South America or somewhere leaving Claudio (I already thought of him as Claudio) alive and well was alto- gether beyond me. For the matter of that, from what I al- ready knew or guessed of Claudio, whoever he was, I thought it quite possible that I should not be able to collect the money, still less enjoy it, unless he was put out of the way first, and, as I have said, he was in himself an obstacle I should have no compunction in removing. But the truth is, I found myself already very unwilling to say no to Peter's widow. It was nothing to do with love, not as soon as that. But I admired her and felt for her, and she was not, in any case, an easy woman to say no to. She had tamed Peter, and for wildness I was not in Peter's class.

I did not say, as Benedick does, "Ha, not for the wide world," but I do not suppose for a moment that I looked anything but startled, and then for the first time she smiled at me with real warmth in her smile.

"Oh, come," she said. I still had not said anything, but she answered the look on my face. "It won't be the first man you've killed, and he deserves it if anyone does. I mean, I'd kill him myself if I could, but you're much better qualified to do it than I am."

Perhaps because I could not yet think what I wanted to

say, I came out with the obvious practical objection. "I don't know who he is," I said.

She was still smiling, but gently, so that I felt like an unreasonable small boy. "No," she said, "no, there's that. But you'll have Peter's letter. He only uses initials, but it may help you to remember." She had stopped smiling now, and was looking at me very straight. "In any case," she said, "when you go off after whatever it is, I'd be surprised if you didn't find him fairly close beside you. Not behind you with a knife—or not until you've actually found it. He needs you until then. But fairly close, all the same, unless you can shake him off. And you can't do that until you know who he is, and once you know that, it's up to you isn't it?"

She was so gently reasonable about the whole thing that I still answered her with reasonable argument. "Why should he come after me?" I said. "He can't know about Peter's letter. He'll think the secret's dead with Peter."

She shook her head. "He'll be afraid of that," she said, "but he can't be certain. For the matter of that, he can't be certain you and Peter weren't already in touch. I mean, Peter could have written to you. He'll be ready to suspect something of the sort because that would account for your coming here in the first place. We know it's pure chance, but he's not likely to believe that. It's much the less likely explanation of the two. In any case, he won't be satisfied. He won't let you out of his sight until he's certain you're not going after it, and if he's the man I take him for, it will take a long time to satisfy him on that. He'll be at a tactical advantage at first—I mean, if you can't remember him even after seeing Peter's letter—but, as I say, he can't use it. Whereas with your experience you ought to be able to flush him out at some point, and then so far as you're concerned he's immediately expendable." She thought for a moment. Then she

23

said, "For the matter of that, he may already know you're here with me now, and if so, he'll know you're on to something. But I don't think so. I doubt if he's had time to get himself organised that far. In any case, you mustn't come here again. If there's anything you want to ask me, there's always the post. He can't intercept letters."

I was over my surprise now. I was past being surprised at anything in Peter's widow. I sat back in my chair and fairly laughed at her, and to her enormous credit she laughed back. I said, "It's a pity you didn't go into business with Peter. You'd have made a formidable team. You think of everything, don't you?"

"I did," she said. "Once. I was in with some pretty bad people too. That was how I met him. After that I pulled out and took him with me. And yes, since you mention it. We worked very well together, in that and in everything else." She was no longer smiling now. She was completely serious and entirely committed, as I had seen her at the funeral. "Well?" she said.

I said, "I must think," but she shook her head, and smiled again. She looked at me, that damned smiling woman, and said, "Fie, my lord, fie, a soldier and afeared?"

That was too much. I had known Peter for a fellow bardo-later, but I had not expected her to be one. I suppose he had infected her over the years. I have always found that particular wifely stab specially unnerving, because we never hear it actually delivered at MacBeth, but only recalled as part of Lady Macbeth's somnambulant indiscretions, so that it has the effect of suggesting a whole series of marital arguments, perhaps, like those of Bishop and Mrs. Proudie, hidden behind the bed-curtains. At any rate, I made Macbeth's response to another, similar rebuke. I said, "I dare do all that may become a man," but I did not add Macbeth's gloss on the statement. It had not, after all, done him much good, and I did not for a moment suppose it would help me.

"Well, then," she said. "And there is the money, after all. I don't suppose, from what he said of you, that you've had Peter's opportunities of making money. You can use it, can't you?"

"I need it," I said, "very badly indeed."

She nodded. "There's no time to think," she said. "You must take the letter and go now, and then you're committed, aren't you? I'm not putting that in the post, and I'm not keeping it here. I'm much too vulnerable. You must see that."

"And supposing I can't make head or tail of it?"

She shook her head very firmly. "I don't believe that," she said, "not for a moment. It's fairly detailed, and it's about something you were in on."

"I see," I said. "Why do you suppose Peter left it? Or indeed wrote it in the first place?"

"But that was just like Peter. He was a great one for writing things down. He kept a diary up to the time we got married. Did you know that? All through his Establishment days, and even later. I never saw it, but I think it would have been good reading. But it was dynamite, of course, at least so far as Peter was concerned, and when we got married, he burnt it. He didn't keep any more diaries after that. There was nothing to record." And then suddenly and shatteringly the while mask cracked, and a big tear ran down each side of her nose. But she still did not turn away or do anything about them. "I'm sorry," she said. "I didn't mean to do that. It happens sometimes when I don't watch it. But I didn't mean to do it to you."

I said nothing, but I did not at all like the way I felt. Then she said, "But I think there may have been another reason

25

too. I think he may in some way have been making provision for me. I knew all about you, of course, and if the need had been bad enough, I could probably have got in touch with you somehow. And the letter itself would mean nothing to anyone who didn't know what it was about." She thought for a moment. "What will you do with it?"

We were back on a business footing again, and I answered without hesitation. "Oh, burn it," I said. "Memorise and burn. It's a trick I have. James Bond stuff. I don't think Peter had it. He wouldn't if he had this passion for writing things down. I shan't set fire to it with a gold-plated lighter, or whatever it was James Bond used. I'll just put it in the fire once I'm sure of it."

She nodded. "Good," she said. "Will that take long?"

"I don't know till I've seen it, obviously. In any case, I won't do it here."

She nodded again. "All right, if you're sure. You can look after it, and yourself, until then?"

I got up. "I reckon so," I said. "As you say, I doubt if Claudio's got himself organised that far yet. Let me have it, and I'll be off."

She frowned at that. "Claudio?" she said.

"Never mind," I said. "Just a name."

She said nothing, but I could see her mind working, and I thought she'd be on to it presently. Then she got up too and made a move to the door, but stopped and turned again. "Have you got a gun?" she said.

"Only a shotgun," I said. "Legal and surprisingly effective, only you can't carry it around with you. It's up at the cottage."

"You'd better have Peter's," she said. "He kept one. Illegal, of course. I'll get that, too."

"What about you?" I said.

26

"I don't need it. I'm not much good with them, anyway. I take refuge behind total and genuine ignorance. That's once the letter is in your hands."

I hesitated, but the thought of the long dark walk up to the cottage with Peter's letter in my pocket persuaded me. You could not get a car within a quarter of a mile of the cottage. You left it in a shed at the bottom of the hill and walked up. That was one of the things that had attracted me to the cottage in the first place, but now the idea seemed less attractive. And in any case I had to kill Claudio with something. "All right," I said, "thank you," and she turned and went out.

I took another look round that warm, pleasant room and then made for the bookshelves. When people own books, which mostly they do not these days, the books they have can tell you almost all you need to know about them. But before I got there, the door opened and she was back again. She had an envelope in one hand and a cardboard box in the other. "There they are," she said.

I put the envelope into the inside pocket of my jacket. The box I put on a table and opened. The gun was a Colt 38 automatic—not, again, James Bond stuff, but they work. It had been beautifully kept. There were some loose cartridges with the gun and a small square box of fifty, which by the weight of it was full. I slid the magazine out of the butt. It was empty. I topped it up with the loose cartridges, worked the slide to bring one up into the chamber and then put another round into the top of the magazine and put the safety-catch on. No use doing things by halves. I dropped the remaining two or three loose cartridges into my trouser pocket and put the box of fifty into a side pocket of my jacket. The gun for the moment I kept in my hand. She watched me in silence. When I had finished, she said, "All right?"

27

"Fine," I said. I had put my overcoat over a chair, but now I put it on and dropped the gun into its right-hand pocket. "Ready," I said.

She nodded, and we went out together into the hall. Inside the front door we stopped and turned and looked at each other. I said, "I expect you know my name. May I know yours?"

"I know you as Ben," she said. "My name's Lisa."

"Lisa Gaston," I said. "I can't even think of you as Mowbray, let alone Peter."

She gave me a quick, faint smile. "I wouldn't want you to," she said, "only don't use it."

"Not to anyone but you," I said, "and even then not on paper. So the occasion may not arise."

She said, perfectly seriously, "I hope it will. But not until the thing's done. You can write if you need to. Or even phone. Mowbray's in the book. But I'd rather you wrote. I don't like the phone. But only if you have to, either way. In present circumstances, I mean."

I said, "I know exactly what you mean." For a moment we looked at each other very gravely. Then I said, "All right. Let me out quickly and lock up after me. Good-bye, Lisa."

She put out a hand suddenly, and I took it and held it for a moment. It was like her, very cool and hard, but with a lot of life under the skin. We did not actually shake hands. I just held her hand for a moment. Then she said, "Good-bye, Ben," and I let go her hand, and she opened the door and I went out.

There was no porch-light on now, only the street lighting, adequate but not brilliant. I stood and looked up and down the street, and as I looked, I heard the door shut quietly behind me and the latch-lock click shut. I waited until my eyes had adjusted themselves to the dimness, and then I walked

28

to the gate. It was still early in the evening. Most of the houses had lights behind drawn curtains, but there was no one about. It was very quiet. I looked both ways before I went out, but there was not the cover for a cat. In any case, if Claudio knew his business, as I felt sure he did, he would be by the car, or even in it. I went out of the gate and set out briskly towards it with my right hand in the pocket of my coat. My nerve had been good enough in the old days, but I was twenty years older and out of practise. I reminded myself that I was no use to Claudio dead, only I knew that with the letter in my pocket this was not in fact true, and then I had to tell myself that he could not know about the letter, and even if he suspected it, he could not risk precipitate action.

I saw no one all the way to the car, and when I got to it, there was no one near it or inside it. It was under a street lamp, and I could see enough to be sure. I got in and drove back to the shed at the foot of the path up the hill. I had the headlights now, and there was no cover here either, but there was still no one waiting for me. I put the car away and turned out the lights. The darkness was absolute, and so was the silence. There was no street lighting here and no lights behind drawn curtains. There was not a house for a mile or two in any direction except the cottage a quarter of a mile up the path. I got out of the car and groped along its side to the door of the shed, and there too I stood and waited until my eyes were at full stretch. I had a torch, but I was not going to use it. I waited a minute or so and then set off up the path.

I did not at all enjoy the walk up the hill to the cottage. It was the first of several such walks I took with Claudio, and I never found them anything but trying. After a bit, of course, I got used to them, as you get used to living with a chronic pain, but whether the evil is pain or fear, tolerance is a poor substitute for relief. Whether he was really there I have no idea, any more than I had on half the other walks I took with him. I should think, now, that it was very unlikely. But it was my first walk with him, and a very dark, lonely one, and dead quiet. I took it very slow, stopping in my tracks every now and then to look and listen behind me. In that silence I could not really believe that I should not hear him, but he had caught Peter, and Peter, when I had known him, had had the hearing of a red deer. I suppose even a man like Peter loses his edge in time, and of course his mind would have been on me ahead of him and not on Claudio behind him. All the same, it had been a most uncharacteristic way for him to die. So I went, as I say, very slowly and carefully, and I saw and heard nothing all the way.

It was only when I could make out the dark shape of the cottage ahead of me that I took the torch out of my pocket with my left hand. I already had the gun in my right, and the safety-catch was off. I stopped and turned and swept the beam of white light in a quick semi-circle behind me, but there was no one there and nowhere where anyone could be. Then I turned again, and with torch and gun both pointing ahead I advanced on the cottage. I went all round it once, shining the torch all round me as I went. Then I went round it again, shining the torch in through the windows, very carefully and methodically. I had left all the curtains open. You do not leave curtains drawn when you have to come back into a place. Still no Claudio. I went to the door, dowsed the torch and dropped it into my coat pocket. Even after the torch-light, the darkness seemed unbelievably dense. I fumbled in my trouser pocket for the key, sorting it out carefully from the few loose cartridges that were in the pocket with it. I did not want to lose a single one. I did not

have very many of them, and I did not know where I could
get any more. I could have done with a spare magazine as
well, but I should need that only in a prolonged gun-fight,
and I did not really anticipate that. Then I opened the door
and went in and locked the door behind me.

I groped all round the cottage in the dark, drawing the
curtains close on all the windows. Then at last I put on the
lights, and in their yellow glow the place looked harmless
enough, though I went all over it to make sure. I put the gun
on the table next to my usual chair, and the torch with it,
and took off my overcoat and hung it up, and let myself relax
a little. I did not really think Claudio was in the
neighbourhood now. I made up the fire, an old-fashioned
coal fire in an open grate, though I wondered who had
brought the coal up from the road. Then I settled myself in
my chair and took Peter's envelope out of the inside pocket
of my jacket.

CHAPTER 4.

As I say, I reckoned I had nerve enough, or had had, but that was on dry land. Water scared the wits out of me, and always had. I do not know why. No doubt a traumatic experience I had been careful to forget, or even, on an older view, something that had happened to my mother during pregnancy. Anyway, there it was. I had learnt to swim, of course, partly because it is expected of you, and partly because I knew that if I did not, I should be even more scared of water than I should be if I could swim. But I never swam except of necessity. Not for me the sunlit summer beaches, or even the municipal swimming-bath. The last time I had swum of necessity (and it had hardly been swimming at that) had been on my last job for the Establishment, and it had been the finishing touch. I signed off after it, and never did another job for them. That, too, I had done my best to forget. It is also, of course, true that at my sort of age it is the things about twenty years back that you do forget. You remember recent things, and you remember things further back than that, but twenty years is just the wrong interval. And now Peter's letter had brought it all back again. It was that last job that the letter was all about.

It had been a straightforward collect-and-fetch job. In all the usual ways it had been almost without incident, but it had ended in disaster through nobody's fault. There had been three of us on the job, Peter in charge, myself and an-

32

other man I could not remember, except that I had a distinct
impression that I had rather liked him. This was odd, because on the evidence he must have been Claudio, who had
just tried to kill me. Odder still, his first initial was C. He was
C. T. in the letter, but I could not remember who he was.

We were never told more than was necessary for the effi-
cient performance of the job assigned to us, nor, most of the
time and most of us, did we want to know more. It would
not have helped us to do the job better or more safely, and if
the law of the country did catch up with us, a convincing
claim to ignorance of what was involved might help. On that
occasion all we knew was that we had to collect an ex-
tremely valuable consignment and bring it back intact. We
did not have to acquire it ourselves, whatever it was, merely
collect it from a friendly party and get it back, if necessary
against the opposition of other, less friendly parties. We duly
collected it in a foreign country—I am not, even now, saying
which—and got ourselves back to a French port. At one
point we had thought ourselves followed, and Claudio, if it
was Claudio, had been detached to deal with the follower.
He had done so and rejoined the party. All this was run-of-
the-mill.

At the port we had duly introduced ourselves to a couple
of hearty, weather-beaten English yachtsmen. We did not
ask their names, nor they ours. We called them, among ourselves, the navigators. One of them probably owned the boat
with the other as his assistant, and I expect they were well
known amateurs at the local yacht-club wherever they came
from, but were not above doing a little professional sailing
on occasion if the approach was discreet enough and the
price right. My impression is that there are a good many
such, and feeling as I do about sea-faring, I give them my
unbounded admiration. The navigators got us aboard with

33

the utmost discretion, and we retired below and stayed there until they left port at what was no doubt the most probable and convenient time for yachtsmen to sail. Peter presumably had the consignment, whatever it was, about him somewhere, but as I saw no sign of it, I assumed it was very small.

It was a big yacht for two men to handle, at least to my way of thinking, but I know very little about such things. At any rate, the navigators gave an impression of both competence and confidence, and I left the worrying to them. I think probably they could have done with more hands, but found it better in the circumstances to keep the thing to themselves. They were not, in fact, due to take us all the way to England. In case the yacht had been identified in her French port, and could be met on arrival, we were to rendezvous off the coast with another boat, which would get us ashore at the appointed place, while the jolly yachtsmen made a leisurely voyage to a by then innocent landfall at their home port, wherever that was. I can only assume that the considerable complication of the arrangements reflected the value of the cargo carried. In any case, before we had been half an hour at sea I stopped worrying about anything but my own misery. It would have been a proper irony if an anti-sailor like myself had been immune from sea-sickness, just as Lord Nelson (not to mention Captain Hornblower) had been a prey to it, but even that mitigation was denied me. In point of fact, I doubt if it would have been any mitigation. All these jokes about sea-sick passengers hoping the ship will sink may be an exaggeration, but the exaggeration is a permissible one. I can only say that up to the final crisis I felt no fear, whereas in any other physical condition except complete unconsciousness I should have been scared out of my wits. I was conscious of the violent movement of the yacht, but only as the cause of my own devastation. We had, in fact, run into appalling conditions, but I suppose the necessity of keeping their appointment prevented the navigators from running for shelter, if there was any shelter to run to, until it was too late.

At some point in my eternity of suffering the ship struck. There was a tearing crash, followed by a few moments of comparative silence and then a far worse crash. Everything went sideways and stayed there. The yacht had stopped moving, and the sea was hitting it with the solid, repetitive blows of a battering ram. A moment later the hatch was thrown back and one of the navigators bellowed for all on deck. The other two went up and I stayed where I was, too stupid with sea-sickness to move. Presently one of the navigators came down and yanked me to my feet and got a lifejacket over my head. Fear had now got the better of physical prostration, and the fact that the yacht was steady on the rock probably helped. I fastened the jacket as told and went up the steps with him into the bedlam on deck.

The one thing it was not was seriously cold (it was in very late summer, in fact), and this was probably the saving of those of us who did survive. Otherwise it was pitch-dark overhead, and so far as I could see in any direction, which was not far, there was nothing but white breaking water. The roar of wind and sea was so enormous and continuous that all speech was inaudible unless it was bellowed next to your ear. The yacht was cocked up sideways on the rocks, and on one side there seemed to be rocks everywhere with that lunatic sea breaking over them and smashing away at the exposed side of the boat. There had been no water apparent below when I came up, and if she was holed, it could not have been serious. She was not going to sink, she was simply going to be broken up where she lay. With the iron hull of a sizeable ship this might have taken hours or even days, but with a small wooden hull it was more likely a matter of minutes. The mast had snapped off a few feet above the deck, and the wreckage was lying over the side towards the rocks. We carried a rubber dinghy, one of those things that look like a big bath-tub with balloon sides. It was used as the ship's tender, and the navigators had got us aboard in it when the yacht was moored in the middle of the harbour. But it had taken only three at a time, even in those conditions. It was tied on the roof of the cabin, and one of the navigators was working on it as I came up. I can still remember the spurt of incredulous admiration I felt, in my own total panic, at the apparently deliberate way he was going about whatever he had to do. The other navigator gripped me by the arm and bundled me along towards the bow. The deck was slippery and sloping, but steady enough. He pointed to a wooden life-raft and yelled instructions for getting it loose and fastening myself to one side of it. It was not the sort of thing you could get onto. You merely tied yourself to the side of it and trusted to it to keep you afloat. He left me there and went back, and I struggled desperately and not very efficiently to do what he had told me. A moment later he was back with Claudio, and pointed him to the other side of the raft. Between us we got the raft clear and the two of us tied to it with loops of rope under our armpits. For obvious reasons, Claudio and I were by now more or less flat on the deck and only the navigator was on his feet, crouching by us in the general bedlam. He gave us our sailing orders in an entirely matter-of-fact sort of way that was most effective in the circumstances. He said, "Over the side with you, then. Kick yourselves clear of the ship if you can, and then the sea will take you ashore, if you can live that long. Good luck to you." Then he set us sliding, and a moment later we were in the water.

I do not remember much about our journey ashore, except that we did get there. It was mostly a matter of trying to get enough air to breathe between the clouds of water that broke over us almost continuously. I have no idea how long it lasted. It seemed an eternity, of course. I only remember that soon after we were in the water, I was conscious of a light shining on my face, and found that some sort of a signal lamp had been switched on automatically and was flashing at intervals, presumably to guide rescuers to us if there had been any rescuers about, which there were not. Very ingenious, all the same, and very well-intentioned, however useless in the circumstances. The one thing it did do, as I realised only now for the first time, was to guide Peter to us, but only when we were all three of us ashore—or nearly. During our long drift to the shore it showed me, at intervals, Claudio's white face and staring eyes opposite me, and presumably showed mine to him, but we made no attempt to communicate, each wholly occupied with his individual struggle for survival. At some point I found, almost incredulously, that the sea was breaking over us less frequently and violently, so that I began to take breathing almost for granted. We still rose and fell as the waves went under us, but they were driving us steadily along with them. I wondered, in my new-found hope of survival, if I was going to be sea-sick again, but decided I was not. Then at some point Claudio gave a sort of strangled yelp, and a moment later my dangling feet touched bottom under me.

We began simultaneously, as if under the orders of an unseen navigator, to get ourselves free of the raft before it turned over in the surf, and we must have managed it at much the same moment. By then we were no more than up to our waists in water—between waves. The waves still broke over our heads and shoulders as they drove us up the beach,

37

but it was firm sand under us, and we both kept our feet. There was a real touch of grey now in the sky ahead, and as the water got shallower, I could see a shimmer of wet sand beyond the seething spume that washed about our legs. Of the land itself I could still see nothing. Then for the first time we spoke to each other.

Claudio suddenly pointed ahead and said, "Look!" and I saw a dark figure on the edge of the sand, waving to us with both arms above its head.

I saw it only for a moment, and then it disappeared again, but I had no doubt who it was. There was something entirely characteristic in the way it moved. I said, "Peter!" and we both broke into a sort of shambling, water-logged run that carried us out of the last of the surf and on to the beach. At first we could not see him anywhere, and then we found him lying face-down on the sand, and could not rouse him at all. The enormous surge of relief I had felt at the sight of him suddenly went cold on me, but when I felt his heart I knew he was still alive, though apparently quite unconscious. I could not understand how he could be on his feet and waving at one moment and out cold the next. It was only later that I found a lump the size of a pigeon's egg on one side of his head, and realised that he was heavily concussed. Concussion can do that to you, leaving you on your feet for quite some time after you have had the knock, and then suddenly hitting you like a pole-axe. We were neither of us in much shape ourselves, and Claudio had only one hand in use, but we dragged him up the beach somehow, and all the time the grey light was getting stronger. We dragged him up the sand until it turned into a steep pebble beach, and then we could get him no further. We settled him on the stones as comfortably as we could and of necessity, because it was essential to the job, went over him, looking for what he had been carrying. We found nothing, but his jacket was gone, and I assumed that, whatever it was, the thing had gone with it.

I was now in acting command. There was always an order of seniority laid down for all parties sent out from the Establishment, and in this party I was Number Two. I said, "You stay with him. I'll go and get help." I left them there, with Peter flat out on the stones and Claudio crouched beside him, nursing a wrist that was either broken or badly sprained. I myself went on up the beach. When I got to the top, I saw two things simultaneously, both straight ahead. The first was a small hill with what looked like a square tower on top of it. It was simply a black outline against the grey of the sky. The second, much nearer at hand, but still some way ahead, was lights in the windows of a house.

The people in the house were magnificent. Perhaps it was not their first experience of the sort. The wife got on the phone, and the husband and son came back with me down the beach. The three of us got Peter up to the house, with Claudio, helpless with exhaustion and his damaged wrist, staggering alongside. It took us some time, and by the time we got there there was an ambulance and a police car waiting. They loaded Peter and Claudio into the ambulance and shut the doors on them. That was the last time I ever saw Peter alive. I had begun to think by then. I said all I wanted was a bed. Otherwise I said as little as possible, but I did tell them that there were two men still unaccounted for. They put me in the back seat of the police car, and I went to sleep at once. They took me to a small hotel and got me undressed and into bed. I gathered we had come ashore on an island. There are several islands in the sea between France and England, and so far as I am concerned, you can take your pick. I kept myself awake until I thought the police would have gone, and then left my room and asked for a telephone.

I had to assume that the navigators were lost, and obviously I needed more details of them and the yacht before anyone started asking me serious questions. I got through to a number on the mainland. It was a number given to us for use only in an extreme emergency, but the Establishment machinery was in full working order, and I got the information I wanted. Not trusting my memory in the state I was in, I borrowed pencil and paper from the hotel and made notes. Then I went back to bed, put the paper under my pillow and went to sleep. By the time the police returned, as they were bound to do, I was awake and had got the details into my head and washed the paper down the water-closet. I gave them a reasonable story and asked for news of the navigators. They said one body had been washed up, and the other man was still missing and must be presumed drowned. I asked to be taken to the hospital, where I saw Claudio, in fair shape, but with his arm in plaster. Peter was reported all right, but incommunicado. I gave Claudio the necessary details and my story to the police, and we agreed that I should get back to the mainland at once and report, which I did next day. The gale had blown itself out, but there was a devilish swell, and I was sea-sick again all the way.

That was the end of the incident so far as I remembered it, still unwillingly, twenty years later. Now Peter's letter put an entirely new complexion on the thing, and I sat there in that silent, upland cottage, mercifully far from the sea, wondering what I was going to do about it.

CHAPTER 5.

Peter had written:

When the ship struck, I was carrying the thing in the pouch of a belt worn next to my skin. I had been given the belt with the thing. The thing itself was in a steel box, about 4" x 2" x 1", sealed with solder. It seemed to add very little to the weight of the box. I still do not know what it was, and if you come to read this, it will mean I never shall. If I don't, I hope you will. I detailed you and C.T. to the life-raft and myself to the dinghy with the navigators. This was the sort of decision one has to take, and you will understand. I was still at that stage determined to deliver the goods if I could, and you and C.T. were by then, in military terms, expendable. In fact, as you know, I made the wrong choice, but then so did the navigators. When I last saw the raft's light from the yacht, it seemed to be clear of the rocks to leeward, and I thought you had a chance. We got afloat all right in the dinghy, but it capsized almost at once, and we all went into the water. I lost the navigators in a matter of seconds, and as you know they both went down. I did not consciously decide what to do, it was decided for me. The sea threw me on the rocks, and my one idea was to get out of the water and on to something solid. You know the conditions at the time and can imagine what it was like. I got knocked

41

about a lot and nearly drowned in between, but eventually I got myself under the lee of a high spike of rock, with the sea breaking over it, but not coming over green. By now it was getting lighter, and I could see higher rocks along the line of the reef with the sea washing through between. I did not know what the tide was doing, and I had to get to them if I could. I made it by stages, taking the gaps between waves. At a fairly late stage I fell and banged my head badly, but I kept going, and after a bit I realised that the reef was rising to the land. My head was in bad shape, but at some point there was only fine spray blowing over me, and then I felt turf under my feet. It was getting lighter all the time, but I still could not see far. I seemed to be on a very narrow headland, with the sea breaking against it on my right hand, which must have been its western or south-western side. On the other side the sea was running in as surf, and I knew there must be a beach further in. I decided to deposit the thing where I could collect it later. I offer no explanation of this decision. Knowing me, you may not be altogether surprised at it. My muzzy head may have helped, but I suddenly felt the Establishment had had all of me it was entitled to, and I could do better on my own. My only problem was to find somewhere where I could cache the box and be reasonably sure of finding it again. The headland was all rocks standing up out of the turf, and I had to find a place I could recognise. I still could not see more than twenty yards or so in any direction, and there was no question of taking cross-bearings. I was going up a steep slope with grey in the sky almost ahead of me when I saw a rock above me outlined against the sky. It was shaped like a monkey's head. (See sketch.) I cut away the turf under the lower side of the rock, earthed the box about nine inches down and trod the turf back over it. Then I went on along the left (i.e., east or north-east) side of the headland, making for where the beach would be. At some point I took off my jacket and the belt and threw them in the surf. I savaged the belt a bit in case anyone found it, but I don't suppose anyone did, or no one that mattered. In case there was anyone about, my idea was to get into the surf just off the beach and come in out of the sea as if I had swum ashore. I didn't much like the idea, but before I took the plunge, I saw a flashing light moving in on the surf, and I knew that the raft had made it, though whether either of you was still alive was anybody's guess. I abandoned my idea of going into the water myself and simply made for the beach along the headland, so that I could be there when the raft came in. I got onto the sand when it was quite close in, and a bit later I saw the two of you wading ashore. I waved and shouted, and the next moment I passed out cold, and when I came to, I was in hospital. You were away to England before they even allowed C.T. to see me. I assumed you would have looked for the thing and not found it on me, and that you had by now reported it lost, but the moment I saw C.T., I knew something was wrong. I expect you will remember C.T. He had a certain charm and a lot of cunning and was good in action, but he would never have made a poker-player. You could read his thoughts in his face. I know, because one had to remember this in detailing him for particular duties. From the moment we met, he had suspicion written all over him. And there was another thing. He had once seen the belt on me, when we were changing clothes in the cabin after we got on board the yacht, and he must have known that it was not the sort of thing that would come off easily, even in the water. (I had, in fact, been wrong to take it off—I should have kept it on but torn the pouch open.) But there must have been more to it than that, and I wondered later whether I had come round temporarily in the ambulance and done some talking. You will understand that I could remember very little at first and had to put the thing together from bits and pieces as I remembered more. C.T. never said anything to me or apparently to anyone else, but he never let me out of his sight all the rest of our time on the island. He was quite shameless about this. My difficulty was, and remains, that I do not know where we came in. This is not a question of not remembering. I never knew, and I never saw the place by daylight, as you and C.T. must have, and could not therefore recognise it if I saw it again. It must have been somewhere on the north-west side of the island, but you only have to look at the map to see the difficulty. There is a whole series of small headlands with rocks running out from them and other reefs running out between, which no doubt were headlands once before the sea scoured the land off them, and between the headlands and the reefs there are sand beaches all the way along. I never had the chance to ask anyone the right sort of questions. I tried once or twice in the hospital, but probably no one knew, and in any case they kept on telling me not to worry, it would all come back presently. You know what nurses are like. Once I was out of the hospital, I always had C.T. tagging along with his ears flapping until we were off the island. I could have asked you, but by the time I was back, you had gone, and I never caught up with you. I

could have gone after you, but at first I had plenty else
on hand, and later for various reasons I never got
around to it, though I thought of it more than once. If I
had gone back by myself, I might have spent weeks or
months looking for that damned rock and still not found
it. With you there to identify the headland, we should
have had a very good chance, but that never happened.
If you read this, you should have a good chance too,
even by yourself. You should be able to find the right
headland, and then it's just a question of looking for the
monkey's head. But watch out for C.T. If he has any
idea you're after it, he'll be after you. He can't find it
without you, but if you find it, watch out. Anyway,
good luck.

I had told Lisa Gaston I would memorise Peter's letter,
and I did, partly to show myself I still could, and partly because I did not want to fall short in any way of the promises
I had made her. I cannot say I had any real idea at that stage
of the difficulties this was going to land me in later, but I already had a feeling that the bargain was a tight one, and that
she had already discharged the whole of her side of it. At
any rate, I reckon that if I could compare the version of
Peter's letter I have set down with the original text, there
would be very few discrepancies, and those of no significance. In point of fact, of course, all I needed to remember
could be put down in a couple of lines. I did consider making a copy or tracing of Peter's marginal sketch, which by
itself could mean nothing to anyone, but I decided against
even that. It was nothing more than everyone's mental picture of a monkey's head, with the round dome on top and
the round prognathous jaw-line sticking out below it. The
important thing about it was that it faced left, like the

present sovereign's head on the postage stamps, though like it, I hasten to say, in no other respect. I am a royalist to my backbone. This would have been as Peter had seen it from below as he faced roughly eastward. It had not been far from the autumn equinox when the wreck happened, and the sun would be rising nearly due east, though the dawn pallour might start a bit north of that. The ideal thing would be to repeat Peter's experience in detail, short of, decidedly well short of, getting in the water. As we were now past the equinox, this would put my attempt nearly a year ahead, unless I was going to go at once, and there were several good reasons against that. The obvious one was that Claudio might be expecting me to go at once, and the longer I put it off, the more likely he would be to think that I had no reason to go at all. But there were other considerations as well. For one, I had a job, and with no technical qualifications except largely extra-legal ones, I had not found jobs easy to come by. I could live, just, on my job for another ten months or so, and then take my annual holiday at roughly the same time of the year, which would be on the face of it unsuspicious, as might even be a decision to spend it, although off-season, on an island that was, after all, a recognised holiday resort. If I found the thing, I might or might not live in happy affluence ever after, but until I knew more of my chances, I was unwilling to put myself in the position of having to live by my wits, or on welfare, or on a mixture of the two. Also, I had the police to think of, not only Claudio. They could not in the circumstances prevent me from leaving here and going back to London at the end of my fortnight's holiday, but they might well ask their London colleagues to keep an eye on me for a bit, and if the first thing I did when I got back was to set about leaving the country, it would certainly put ideas in their heads. The last thing I wanted was to have the island police regarding me as an object of interest from the moment I landed. All in all, the thing was better left, though I thought I would write to Lisa and explain my reasons for the delay. It is curious, looking back, to think how much I already felt I was working to her orders rather than carrying out my side of an equal bargain.

Meanwhile, I put Peter's letter in the fire at some time after midnight and was conscious of a sense of relief as soon as I had done so. There was now, finally, no reason for Claudio to kill me unawares, as he had once tried to do, and even thought he had done, and every reason why he should keep me alive, at least for a limited time, and while there is life, there is hope. The information he needed was stored in my brain and nowhere else, and in the present state of science (though no doubt things will improve) you cannot get at information stored in a man's brain unless that brain is still alive. Already you can store a man's heritable qualities in frozen sperm, though you still have to risk crossing them with those of another person, and may not, at least at a first attempt, get the ones you want. But as things are now, what a man has acquired in his lifetime dies with him, and that includes a fair part of what he knows. I still had to risk Claudio's appearing at my bedside with ropes and a cigarette lighter, and burning the information out of me (and I had never for a moment seen myself as the sort of man who would retain information for very long in such circumstances), but this was far easier to guard against than a knife in the back, and to that extent my position had improved. So I put Peter's letter in the fire, took my routine precautions against surprise attack and went to bed, and slept as soundly as my rapidly reviving mental alarm system permitted.

I awoke reasonably refreshed, and set about a course of action which, though directed to what was now my main ob-

jective, at least lacked urgency, and was proportionately easier to live with. After breakfast I wrote to Lisa Gaston
explaining my decision in terms that I knew she would understand, but that would read harmlessly enough to anyone
(other than Claudio) who happened to get hold of the letter.
I dated the letter as from my London address, which she had
not got, though it was certainly known to Claudio and the
police. I did not examine too closely my reasons for doing
this, but I think the truth is that I wanted to know that she
could resume touch with me if for any reason she decided to.
I had no telephone of my own in London. I did not live on
that sort of scale. I took my letter down to Brancastle and
posted it at the head Post Office. From there on it was more
likely to suffer from the vagaries of the postal service than
from what the Prayer Book calls the assaults of our enemies.
But against the postal service we are all equally unprotected.

After that I simply went on with my holiday, and in a reasonably carefree state of mind, which I hoped both Claudio
and the police would take note of. On consideration I had
come to the conclusion that it was almost certainly myself
that Claudio had been keeping an eye on, not Peter. It is
much easier, if you know the ropes and are unscrupulous
enough, to keep an eye on someone in a wilderness of
London bed-sitters than in a place like Brancastle, and I was
an easy person to keep an eye on, because my movements
were so restricted. I was regular in my employment and
went on holiday only once a year. He must have monitored
my holidays, and may even have followed me until he was
satisfied where I was going. It did my heart good to imagine
his excitement and self-congratulation when he found I was
at last heading north for the neighbourhood of Brancastle.
He would presumably keep an eye on me as long as I stayed
there, and would then, with a resignation it gave me equal

48

pleasure to think of, go back to his London arrangements, which almost certainly involved one or more of my neighbours in the place where I lived. I could think of three or four of them who would be happy to supply a little simple information against a modest regular retainer, and I had no doubt some of them did.

The local police never came near me during the rest of my time at the cottage, though I have no doubt they made it their business to know I was still there. Nor did I have any further contact with Lisa Gaston, though she would have had my letter, and knew I was not yet in London. When my fortnight was up, I left all in order and drove down to Brancastle. I went first to the police station, where the sergeant on duty thanked me for calling, with the usual deadpan politeness, and wished me a pleasant drive home. Then I dropped the keys of the cottage at the agency where Peter had worked, and would still be working if I had never come there, and set off for London.

CHAPTER 6.

I lived in a single room in a building entirely given over to such rooms. If this sounds sordid, it probably was, but I have never attached much importance to my actual living quarters or been ready to spend much money on them. If you have other people to consider, children especially, you obviously cannot view the thing with this sort of detachment, but apart from one relatively short and almost totally disastrous episode, I had lived all my adult life alone. The sort of area you live in, your geographical surroundings, I think of immense importance—in particular, I do not believe that the human mind can survive indefinitely undamaged in purely urban surroundings—but given your surroundings, your personal quarters, the place you hole up in and use for eating and sleeping, seem to me to need little more than basic physical convenience.

This was perhaps especially so in my case, because I used my room for little more than sleeping, and that during the day. I worked as night-watchman at a medium-sized factory in the inner suburbs. I preferred to call myself a night-watchman because that was what, in fact, I was, and I liked the picture the words conveyed of a man going his rounds with a swinging lantern and stick, or even dozing over a brazier in a wooden box, ready to be knocked on the head by any interested intruder. My employers called me Night Security Officer, and I can only suppose paid me accordingly. I had in fact a small room of my own on the ground floor, and some quite complicated electronics in my charge and at my disposal. They were pretty sharp on security. They did not, as far as I knew, go in for government contracts and classified equipment, but they did precision engineering in a highly competitive field, and when they had anything new on the stocks, which half the time they had, they wanted it kept well under wraps until they were ready to launch it. So I spent my nights there, and got a canteen supper when I came on duty and a canteen breakfast before I left in the morning, and why therefore should I need a room with a view and an eye-level grill, let alone a *bijou* bachelor *pied-à-terre* with American-style kitchen and a bidet in the bathroom? I had other, better things to spend my money on, what there was of it, and had in any case no one that mattered to see how I lived once I got home in the mornings and shut the door on myself. But I had, once or twice lately, found myself wondering what the end of it was to be, and even facing the fact that I had to make some real money some time. The trouble was that I was becoming increasingly solitary in habit—its isolation was the great attraction of my present job—and found it difficult to imagine any way of making money that did not involve getting mixed up again with other people. No wonder I had accepted Lisa Gaston's proposal, even when I had come to understand its full terms. It was, quite simply, my only way out.

I came up the concrete stairs (there was a lift, but I seldom used it) with my cases in my hand, wondering which of my neighbours was on the look-out for my return. There were, inevitably, several of them that I passed the time of day and exchanged minimal news with, coming in as often as not just when they were going out. These were old inhabitants of the block like myself, stable elements in a population

that for the most part had a fairly rapid turn-over. Now that
I came to think of it, they were a slightly seedy bunch, and
presumably shared with me either an inability to find anything better or a resigned acceptance of living conditions
which the more migrant inhabitants sooner or later found in-
tolerable. Also, though this was a fact I did not particularly
relish when I came to recognise it, they were all people of a
certain age, though still in most cases a good deal older than
myself. I knew their names. Names at least were common
property in the block, because of the big name-board in the
entrance hall. I knew very little else about them because I
had never bothered to find out. Some of them, or at least one
of them, clearly knew a good deal more about me. I did not
grudge them the knowledge, which in all conscience was
harmless enough. I did not even grudge them the pittance
they were probably paid for passing it on. They had presumably been given some story to justify the deal, presumably
by Claudio acting the part of a private enquiry agent seedy
enough to be operating in this sort of setting.

But now that I knew they existed, I found I wanted to
know who they were, and even on consideration decided
that it would do no harm if I let my suspicion of them show
a little. At least it might impair their effectiveness as reporting agents, and this might shake Claudio's confidence in his
arrangements, especially if they reported that I was doing
nothing unusual, which was what I should be doing. To
shake his confidence was a first step towards flushing him
out into the open, which, as Lisa Gaston had said, I had to
do some time. Not knowing them, I could not be sure
whether they would report my apparent suspicion to Claudio. It was certainly something they ought to report, but to
report it might be talking themselves out of a job, which
they presumably set some store by. If they did not report it,

it would still, as I saw it, be to my advantage that they knew of it. If they did, it would suggest to Claudio that I knew something, and then my total failure to do anything about it would upset him all the more. Peter had described him as cunning, but the very choice of word suggested that he was no intellectual giant, and in this sort of psychological warfare, and with nearly a year to play it in, I reckoned I ought to be able to run rings round him.

As it happened, I was rushed into action by meeting one of my possibles as I walked along the dusky passage from the head of the stairs to the door of my room. This was an immensely dignified Oriental called Mr. Ram Chandra. He had that air of enormous other-worldliness which your elderly Hindu so often has, and which I assume is not incompatible with a sharp interest in practical affairs and a beady eye for the main chance. Mr. Ram Chandra and I bowed to each other, as we always did, with the elegance of two full-rigged ships rendering passing honours. He said, "Good morning, Mr. Selby. Back from your holiday?"

I said, "Good morning, Mr. Ram Chandra. Yes, you can tell them I'm safely home. Though, in point of fact, I think they already know."

He inclined his head again, but did not pause at all as we went past each other. Then he hesitated and turned, and found that I had stopped too and was watching him. His high brown brow wrinkled slightly with a sort of courteous bewilderment, and he said, "Excuse me, I do not quite understand. Do you wish me to inform someone of your return?"

I smiled at him, and got in return a full dose of oriental inscrutability. "No, no," I said, "don't worry. I'm sure they'll find out soon enough." For a moment or two we stood there looking at each other, and for the life of me I could see noth-

ing in his face but the same slightly pained bewilderment.
Then he bowed again and turned and went off along the passage towards the stairs. I found myself also bowing to his re-
treating back, and then I pulled myself up and went on and
let myself into my room.

I had the day to spare before I returned to duty at the
works in the evening. I mean, of course, that I always had
the day to myself, but now there was no need to sleep, because I had had a full night's sleep at a hotel half-way back
from Brancastle. I could perfectly well have left early and
done the journey in one piece, but I like my journeys leisurely. Also, like many other people who look after themselves, I enjoyed hotels, briefly, for their own sake, and they
did not upset my sense of privacy, because a single room in a
hotel is by common consent one of the loneliest places on
earth, so that for a short time I had the best of both worlds.

I decided to spend part of the day buying and fitting an
additional lock to the door of my room. The lock provided
by the management was of the sort anyone with experience
could open by breathing on it from the proper angle. Also,
the management, no doubt, had their own key for it, or a
pass-key, and from what I knew of them could no doubt be
persuaded to lend it briefly to a suitable applicant. Hitherto
this had never worried me. I had had no secrets to hide, and
there was nothing of value in the room except my shotgun,
which was so unlikely a possession in a place like this that no
one would be likely to come looking for it. Now I had Peter's
pistol, and I did not want Claudio, whatever he was looking
for, to deprive me of that. In any case, I did not want him
coming at all, because I did not want him or anyone else
poking about the place, even if he found nothing (and a pistol, unlike a shotgun, is at least fairly easy to hide). I should
have preferred a good mortice lock, but to fit one would in-

volve too much work on the door, and in particular too much noise, so that I settled for a fairly advanced latch-lock, which would involve nothing noisier than a bit-and-brace and a screwdriver. For the comparatively quick work needed on the outside of the door I could count on the dead hours of the day when there was never anyone about in the passage, and the slight change in the outside appearance of the door would with any luck escape attention, especially in the prevailing lack of light.

I did, of course, have occasional visitors to my room, but only at my invitation and in my company. My solitary habit did not extend to a neglect of my physical needs, and I had established friendly relations with one or two reasonably honest members of the profession who were glad to come home with me on occasion, especially in the mornings, when business was normally slack. But I did not want uninvited visitors in my absence, and a good lock was the obvious answer. So I went out to buy one, and it was as I was going down the second flight of stairs that I met Mr. Jessel.

Mr. Jessel lived on the floor below me, but was on the whole my prime suspect. He wore falsity like a garment. I never knew what his occupation was, or indeed if he had one. From his manner he might have been an actor or a British Council officer, but if he was an actor, he must have been a very bad one. His dignity was assumed as clearly as Mr. Ram Chandra's was native to him, and there was nothing I would not have suspected him of unless it called for bold and decisive action. His manner to me was always that of one distressed gentleman to another, as if we were two aristocratic French *émigrés* compelled by political circumstances to lodge in eighteenth-century Fulham. I played along with this because I could not be bothered to do anything else, but now it suddenly irritated me past endurance.

He said, "Ah, Mr. Selby. I trust you found the country air salubrious?"

I am not making this up. He really did talk like that. He was one of the very few people I have known who actually used the word "Ah." I stood and confronted him, so that he was forced to stop too. Not that he minded. I think he rather enjoyed our little encounters, as if they gave him an opportunity to play one of his favourite roles. I said, "Thank you, Mr. Jessel, I did. I found my holiday refreshing, though not without incident, and I have returned in excellent spirits. You are at liberty to report that, if you find it profitable to do so, to anyone who may be interested."

He was clearly frightened, but that may have been nothing more than my sudden undisguised hostility. It would not take much to frighten Mr. Jessel. He actually recoiled from me, not moving his feet, but swaying backwards so far that I thought for one joyful moment that he was going to overbalance and fall downstairs. I had knocked people downstairs in my time, but never with words alone. Then at the last moment he recovered himself, but only by dint of stepping a pace backwards, so that his heels were once more vertically under his head. His anxiety found vent in a high nervous giggle, but his face was all in pieces. He said, "Ah, yes, good. But I assure you, Mr. Selby, that I have no interest in, ah, reporting your movements to anyone."

I said, "Ah, good, Mr. Jessel," and went on down the stairs. This time it was he who stood and watched me go. I listened as I went, and it was quite a time before I heard him go on up the stairs again, breathing as if he had been running. I was still angry, but amused in spite of myself. As an opponent, if he was an opponent, I could not take Mr. Jessel seriously. I took the tube to Soho, where I found the lock I was looking for in the shop I expected would have it. Then,

56

while I was in that rather special shopping area, I decided
suddenly on something else I might profitably buy, and I
went looking for the kind of shop that would have it. I found
it, appropriately enough, next door to a sex boutique, and it
had what I wanted in the window. Genuine Ex-Commando
Daggers, it said. I did not suppose for a moment that they
were genuine. It is an interesting comment on our present culture that it is profitable not only to sell the trappings
of past violence to the people who fancy such things, but
even to manufacture reproductions, as they do with antique
furniture and other graces of a civilisation irretrievably lost.
But I did not worry about their provenance so long as the
steel was good, and this it seemed to be. I tested the edge on
a piece of military brass while the shopkeeper was away
looking for something I asked after but did not want. It
could do with sharpening, but I could attend to that later. I
hesitated, I hoped convincingly, over some pieces of Nazi
uniform, and then paid for the dagger and put the long thin
parcel into the inner pocket of my jacket, from which it
stood up awkwardly almost under my armpit. I had checked
over the short street before I went into the shop, and before
I went fully out I checked it again, perhaps a little casually,
but saw nothing of interest. I walked to the tube station with
the lock in an indeterminate parcel in my hand and the
sheathed knife still pressing against my ribs. I had a belt for
it at home.

So far as Claudio was concerned, I now had two strings to
my bow. One of them I knew he already had. The other I
did not know he had, any more than he knew I had it, but it
was better to assume that he had that too. The remaining
possibility was a blunt instrument for close quarters, and I
felt sure that my supplier next to the sex-boutique, if I asked
him, would have turned up a consignment of genuine Ex-

S.S. Rubber Truncheons, but on reflection I decided against it. There is very little in that line that the human hand, properly taught, cannot do better by itself. The palaeontologists, if those are the people I mean, tell us that the human hand is an advanced, but almost totally unmodified, version of the aboriginal mammalian paw. Unmodified, that is the point. Man never made the mistake other mammals made of physical specialisation. He never grew webs over his fingers like the cetaceans, or a single huge finger like the unguipeds, or even enormous claws like the cats. He kept his five-fingered paw as it was. The only thing he specialised in was brain, and his unspecialised paw directed by his specialised brain has already wiped out most of the rest of creation, and is in a fair way to wiping out himself. In my humble way I was only doing what the super-powers were doing, and seeking parity of armaments with the opposition, but in this particular department of warfare I was content to leave myself with the deadly, undifferentiated mammalian paw.

It was while I was sitting in the tube train on my way home that I felt for the first time that I was being watched. All experienced single-handed hunters, whether they go after man-eating tigers or their own more dangerous kind, agree that this instinct does exist, though its reliability varies. I had experienced it more than once in the old days, and on one occasion at least had proved it right. It could have been right on the other occasions, too, but on the facts as later established I had had to adjudge the thing non-proven. Now after all these years I felt the sensation again. Curiously enough, my first reaction was satisfaction. I had no reason to think I was in immediate danger, and at least it showed that my old capabilities were reasserting themselves, which after all this time I could not assume they would. I did nothing, of course. I was reading the paper, sitting as comfortably as the knife in my pocket allowed, in a carriage which, as usual at that time of day, was more than half empty. I went on reading, or at least moving my eyes backwards and forwards along the lines of print, and let the feeling work on me. As with most things not susceptible of rational explanation, I knew it would not do to let the reasoning mind dwell on it. Man has kept his paw, presumably because his physical experience brought no sufficiently strong pressure to bear to make him modify it, but the enormous and continually growing pressure of his conscious mind has played hell with a lot of his mental and nervous capabilities, and when one of these now vestigial faculties does for a moment reassert itself, your only hope is to shield it as far as possible from the dominant mind. You cannot do this for very long, any more than your waking mind can retain the full significance of a dream. All you can do is to recognise, with your conscious mind, that the thing has happened, and to direct your conscious actions accordingly. I waited until the train ran into a station and then, as almost everyone does, I took my eyes from the paper and watched the people getting in and out. I checked the whole carriage carefully with apparent unconcern. There were not more than fifteen people in it, and I could see no one resembling in any degree the sort of man I was looking for. It was only when the train was moving again that I realised where the watcher could have been. I was sitting near the front end of the carriage, and there was a window in the end wall facing directly into the corresponding rear window of the carriage in front. There was of course no one to be seen through the two windows now, but that was where he must have been, if he existed at all, in the rear end of the next carriage. Unless he had got out at the station, that was where he still was, or at least in that carriage somewhere. I doubted whether he would have another look at me, or indeed whether he would even come all the way to my station. By now he would know well enough where I was going, and I could think of no reason why he should follow me home. What I was concerned with was how far he had followed me in the streets.

I had started out, admittedly, with no thought of being followed at all. I was only going to buy a lock, and I was hoping to buy it from a shop that sold many other things beside locks. Even if my buying and fitting of a lock was known, I could see no harm in it. It was almost bound to be noticed, and presumably reported sooner or later, and it was a purely defensive gesture. My buying of the knife, which I had not originally intended, was a very different matter. Unless you are an expert at knife-play, as some of the Latins are, a knife is not much use as a defensive weapon. To most of us in the Establishment it was a weapon of attack, and specifically of surprise attack. That was how I had used it on the few occasions I had used it, and that was how Claudio had used it on Peter. I did not, as I have said, mind Claudio's knowing that I was consciously on the defensive, but I did not at all want him thinking what was true—that I was consciously on the attack. At best it would make my job very much more difficult. At worst it might alter his own attitudes and intentions. I had to assume that he had a fair respect for my professional capabilities. On the one occasion when I knew I had operated with him, I had been his superior officer, and with the Establishment this indicated a deliberate judgement of superior capacity. Not remembering the man, I had little or no idea how his mind worked, but I had to face the possibility that at some point fear might overcome greed, and he might decide to cut his losses and concentrate on killing me before I killed him. I had nothing firmer to go on than that moment of instinctive apprehension in a moving tube train, but however my conscious mind reasoned, my subconscious accepted what my subconscious had thrown up, and by the time I got out at my station my mental position had decisively changed. I had hitherto rested comfortably on the assumption that I was too valuable to kill. Now I had to face the fact that the assumption, while it might hold good for the present, might not hold good indefinitely, and from then on I was afraid, not badly or all the time, but from time to time in varying degrees.

There were two men in the carriage when I walked past it along the platform who, from what I could see of them, might be Claudio, but I could not see very much of either. Both sat facing me on the opposite side of the carriage, and both had their papers open at full stretch, so that all I could see of them was their legs from the knees down and their hands holding the paper on each side. I had no time for much detail, but I did notice that one of them had very large feet in brightly polished brown shoes and red hands as big as his feet. The shoes cut both ways. It seemed unlikely that a man bent on surreptitious villainy would go around looking like a Cherry Blossom advertisement, especially a man with feet of that size. On the other hand, it was just the sort of detail that a slightly second-rate villain with a touch of vanity might overlook. The train moved past me before I had left the platform, but neither of them had moved. All I could do was to make a mental note of large hands and feet and a touch of showy smartness as possible characteristics of the enemy, and this I did. No one who got out of the train with me was of any interest at all, and I walked home in conscious and slightly relieved solitude. As usual, I went up the stairs, and just as I got to my landing, the door opposite the head of the stairs opened, and Mrs. Iacovou came out. By virtue of proximity and as it were seniority Mrs. Iacovou had to be one of my suspects, but she was not one I was ready, or even very willing, to take seriously. I was rather fond of her, though I had to remind myself that I had possibly been rather fond of Claudio, too. She was a Greek of some sort, perhaps a Cypriot, and she brought a touch of peasantry to our grim urban community. She never wore anything but black. Even her apron was black, and I was prepared to bet that it was a long time since anyone had manufactured and sold a black apron in this country. She was always cheerful, but so far as the rest of us were concerned kept herself very much to herself. Every now and then, especially at week-ends, she was visited by a small tribe of equally cheerful compatriots, and despite the shut doors the whole landing rang with laughter and noisy conversation. What they were all saying I had no idea. As Casca said to Cassius, for my part it was Greek to me. Now she came out of her door alone, and gave me her usual smiling greeting. I said, "Good-morning, Mrs. Iacovou."

She said, "You had a good holiday?"

Almost against my inclination, I gave her a variation of my now standard reply. It was only a mild variation, perhaps slightly puzzling to an innocent mind, but with no shadow of offence in it, but the result was shattering. For a moment she stared at me with her black eyes round with horror, and then she did a thing which temperamental domestics were once said to have done, but which I had never actually seen. She flung her black apron over her head and turned and blundered back into her doorway, slamming the door behind her.

For a moment I stood there as horror-stricken as she was, and then I walked on to my room. I was furiously angry, un-reasonably with myself, but above all with Claudio. If I had had him defenceless in front of me, I would have un-wrapped my knife and used it on him regardless of the consequences. He had tried to kill me once, but that was nothing. Now he had destroyed one of my illusions. I did not have many illusions, and the ones I had I minded about.

CHAPTER 7.

I allowed my anger to cool to a point where I could trust myself not to take it out on either the door or my fingers, and then fitted the new lock to my satisfaction. The satisfaction in its turn completed my mental rehabilitation. Ever since the nicer type of mesolithic man started chipping his microliths with exquisite precision, your craftsman must have had a better time of it than most of us. He has all the satisfaction of the artist without the hang-ups and despair and the meanness of desiring this man's art and that man's scope. I had the temperament, too, that was the funny thing. If my father had apprenticed me to a cabinet-maker, I should not have been half the trouble I have since been to myself or to other people. The snug fitting of my lock contributed more to my sense of security than the working presence of the lock itself. Certainly no one saw me doing it. Whether anyone heard me I doubt. At this time of day there was probably only Mrs. Iacovou near enough at hand, and for all I knew she might still be sitting with her black apron over her ears. In any case, I did not let my mind dwell on Mrs. Iacovou because I did not like to think what might be going on in hers.

I stowed Peter's pistol under a convenient floor-board which I had long known about but never had occasion to use. Then I unpacked and distributed my things and spent a peaceful afternoon letting my mind slip back into its routine

64

processes so as to be ready for going to work in the evening. For all its humdrum nature, my job was a real job which occupied and exercised my mind while I was doing it. When the time came, I went off as usual through crowded streets and the crowded underground, conscious as always of an obscure satisfaction in the fact that the rest of the crowd was coming off work while I was going on. I did not suppose for a moment that Claudio was interested in my going to work, and once I was there, at least if I was doing my job properly, I was free from his attentions. It would be my days that he was interested in, and I thought that so far as I could without undue loss of sleep I might give him something, every now and then, to interest himself in. Nevertheless, I went to work with my knife, already honed to a more workmanlike edge, hanging in its proper place behind my right hip, because that was where, from now on, it belonged, as much a part of my clothing as the braces which in my old-fashioned way I still used to keep my trousers up.

It was a bright breezy day when I came off duty next morning, and I experienced a sense of well-being, as if my holiday really had done me the good it was supposed to have. I even walked a couple of stations before I took to the tube, and it occurred to me that I might bring one of my professional friends home with me, as I often did on the first morning after my solitary holidays. Tamara would be the one, because she was still a cheerful little thing. They give themselves the most remarkable stage-names now, perhaps because there is only a limited number of ordinary names and there are an awful lot of girls. The fact that she pronounced it to rhyme with stammerer rather added to its attractions.

It was with a curious sense of unease that I found I did not particularly want Tamara or any of her friends, and real-

ised, when I came to look at it, that this was something to do
with Lisa Gaston. It was not a romantic feeling at all. It was
certainly not a matter of keeping myself pure for the love of
a good woman. Other things apart, I did not see how Lisa,
on the record, could be classed as that. But she was very
much a real person, which the girls, at least in their professional capacity, could not afford to be. I think the truth was
that after all these years of solitude I had once more been
brought into contact with a lively and dominant mind, and
one which in my present circumstances had a way of being
always with me. If it had been a man's mind, it would have
taken little Tamara in its stride, but it was a woman's mind,
and the woman, whatever else she was and whatever her
feelings were at the moment, was still very much in business
as a woman. I had the feeling that Lisa would not approve of
Tamara, or at least would view her with some degree of sardonic amusement, and me with her when I was with her.
You have to love someone very much, or dislike them very
bitterly, not to find it wiser to abandon your sense of the ridiculous when you are making love to them. I did not either
love or dislike Tamara, indeed I hardly knew her except in
the most restricted and Authorized-Version sense of the
word, and I was afraid Lisa Gaston's sardonic mental presence would be a skeleton at our modest feast. Seeing that
she could not be expected to offer the sort of consolation
Tamara could, I felt this was unreasonable of her, but I had
to admit that it was my doing, not hers. At any rate, I went
home without Tamara, but with an even stronger feeling
that I was now in some curious way Lisa Gaston's man, and
committed to her in a business which, while I recognised its
necessity, I did not particularly relish. As for Tamara and
her colleagues, I had to admit that my need was more for
entertainment than for physical relief. As Hamlet, with a

typically young man's contempt for the tenderer feelings of his elders, pointed out to his mother, the hey-day in the blood was tame, it was humble, or at least was uncomfortably subject to other considerations.

I slept peacefully inside my new lock, free from the fear of the surprise assault and subjugation by Claudio which I had imagined at my remote country cottage, and which if he had the nerve, he could in fact have managed almost equally well on my third-floor landing during the dead hours of the working day. I slept, nevertheless, with the pistol under my pillow, or at least as much under it as comfort would allow. A Colt 38 is a fairly massive piece of metal-work. Routine required that, just as it required me to have my knife at my hip during the day, and you must never neglect routine, especially in a cold-war situation such as this essentially was. My life was, in any case, so much a matter of routine that I had to graft my new requirements onto it, or there was a danger that the routines of peace would blanket the consciousness of fear. This is a danger which, God knows, affects countries easily enough, even though they have separate minds occupied with the separate needs of peace and war. I had only one mind to occupy with both, and I knew it was a danger I must be constantly aware of.

At any rate, routine did re-assert itself, and I found time passing again with the usual unobtrusive speed. It must have been a month or more after my return that I decided to put on an entertainment for Claudio's benefit. This had to be on a Monday because Monday was my free day. Free, I mean, in the special sense I have already explained. I had Sunday night off duty at the works. This meant that when I came off work on a Sunday morning, I could take only the few hours' sleep that met my immediate needs, knowing that I had a full night's sleep ahead of me. On Sunday afternoons I got my weekly exercise by going for a walk, sometimes right out in the country, sometimes on Wimbledon Common or one of the other refuges of the street-bound Londoner. Presumably soothed by this, I went early to bed and got about nine hours' sleep, though, in fact, I have never had the slightest difficulty in sleeping for as long as I have needed when a reasonable opportunity has presented itself. Monday, therefore, was my day for shopping and other business, and of this Claudio was no doubt perfectly well aware. I found it difficult to believe that he supervised all my Mondays or was even in a position to do so, but then I knew so little about him. For all I knew, he might be a night-watchman himself. I supposed it was the sort of work that people with our sort of experience might tend to go in for, though I doubted if he was much above the stick-and-lantern class. At any rate, I could only try.

I prepared and ate my usual Monday breakfast, which was by way of being my weekly exercise in gracious living. The canteen breakfasts, which I ate during the rest of the week were massively sustaining, especially eaten free, but lacked refinement, and the canteen coffee was so awful that I even preferred the canteen tea. When I had finished and cleared up, I walked to Waterloo Station. I walked both so as to do my shopping on the way and so as to give Claudio, if he was interested, the greatest possible chance of observing my movements. Also, I liked to think of Claudio walking to Waterloo in my footsteps. It was quite a way, and I suspected that he was too heavy for walking, and not really dressed for it. In particular, I fancied that his polished shoes, big as they were, were on the tight side. His natural footwear, I felt sure, was army boots, and many of the regular soldiers I had known bought their civilian, off-duty shoes a size too small. But walk he would have to. You cannot tail a

68

walking man in a car any more than you can tail a car on foot. If, in all this, it may be thought that I was putting too much weight on a very partial and speculative observation through a tube-train window, I can only say that my subconscious mind, for which I had a proper respect, insisted on taking it seriously, and in any case it was the only picture of Claudio I had. Reason told me that he could equally well be a small, lithe man with suede ankle-boots and slender white fingers, and I gave reason its due weight. But I had to think of him somehow, and for better or worse I thought of him as the man in the tube. There may, in fact, have been an element of wishful thinking in it, too. Judged in terms of physical menace, I have always found small men more frightening than big men, and small lithe men the most frightening of all. I suspect that man's fight to the top of the animal world was largely motivated by a resentment of the obvious physical superiority of the other species, and this resentment is still responsible for a surprising amount of primitive wickedness in both men and women. I preferred a Claudio with big feet because I saw it as a softer proposition.

I made no attempt on the way there to see if I was being followed because it did not matter very much. I merely hoped I was, because otherwise I was wasting my time. It goes without saying that in the circumstances I could expect no help from the instinctive apprehension I had experienced in the tube train from Soho. That is purely a defence mechanism, a fear that anticipates any conscious reason for fear. It was not going to warn me I was being followed when I wanted to be. As usual, the Enquiries office was busy. I have often wondered who all the enquirers were and what they were enquiring about, but I can never remember making an enquiry at a London terminus without having to wait for it. Now there were three experts on duty, two men and a woman, working with their usual unhurried and massive patience, and producing an astonishing number of answers without the book. I joined the woman's queue because she was much more likely to give me, not now but later, the information I really wanted. She was the type that reaches its peak as a successful barmaid or receptionist not young, but still very conscious of her sex and still deriving a sort of steady, placid satisfaction from even strictly professional dealings with men. There were no women in her queue. The women enquirers were all queueing up for the men. I suspect that no woman ever really trusts another woman to deal with her patiently or even to give her the right answers. It is a handicap all professional women must have to contend with, especially the doctors and the politicians.

When I reached her, I made rather ill-informed but hopeful enquiries, not about the island itself, my island, but about another, smaller island near it, which I knew, not being really ill-informed at all, could be reached only by way of my island. I put a lot of work into that short interview, and it was a rather jolly one. I wanted to establish friendly relations with her if possible, but above all I wanted to make sure she would remember me. It need not be for very long. I left her with an exchange of friendly smiles, a printed schedule of sailings to the island and her advice to write to the island's information office about my journey on from there. I walked slowly out of the office, trying to look lost in thought and at the same time have a quick look at as many as possible of the people in sight. The only reasonable possibility I saw was a man who came to meet me, met me almost face-to-face and passed on with the blank look of a total lack of interest, which from what Peter had said Claudio could never have managed. In any case, I did not really expect to see him. If he had been watching me, he would have no reason to follow me now. He would have other fish to fry, and I wished him joy of it. He might see me, from a distance, safe into the entrance of the Underground, which was what I made for, but he would not come after me.

I went down into the Underground, booked a couple of stations along the home line, travelled my two stages, got out, went above ground and booked myself back to Waterloo again. I did all this at my leisure and got back to Waterloo perhaps half an hour after I had left it. I walked over to the Enquiries office and looked in through the glass doors at the woman's queue. It was still all men, but unless I was very wrong about him, did not seem to contain Claudio. In any case, if he had been there at all, he would be gone by now. I opened the door and went in and took my place at the end of the queue. She saw me when I was still several places from her. She gave me one surprisingly deliberate glance, which clearly recognised me, but gave nothing away, and then returned to her current customer. I moved up the queue with my thumbs pricking. Something wicked this way comes. The man two ahead of me had a complicated enquiry to make, which involved getting out the books on her part and making a good many notes on his, and all the time my sense of apprehension was growing.

When I got to her at last I put on a show of slightly deprecating innocence. I said, "Oh—excuse me, I'm sorry to trouble you. I was in here just now about—" but she cut me off.

"I know," she said. She was looking at me completely deadpan, not with any noticeable hostility, but full of speculation.

I said, "I wondered if by any chance you've had a friend of mine in making the same enquiries. We were going to do

71

the trip together, but we've got into a bit of a muddle, and I can't seem to get in touch with him. He knew I was going to—" but again she cut me off.

"A friend, did you say?" she said.

I nodded and said nothing. I saw her eyes go to the man behind me, and for a moment I too turned and looked at him. He was an African of some sort, dressed in his beautiful national dress, and looking very benign and dignified. The noble savage, I thought, but of course not a savage at all, not half as much as I.

When I turned to her again, she had made up her mind, and when she spoke, it was in almost a confidential whisper. "I don't know about friend," she said. "I thought at first he was a plain-clothes man. Later I didn't." She looked at me very straight. "Look," she said, "it's no business of mine what you're up to and what the two of you are after, but I wouldn't go on holiday with that one, dear, not in your place I wouldn't. I didn't like the look of him. I think you're all right, but I'd keep clear of that one."

I nodded. My mouth was suddenly very dry, but I managed one more question. "Big man?" I said.

She nodded too. "Oh yes," she said, "he was big, all right." Then her eyes went to the African, and she spoke in a normal voice. "Can I help you?" she said.

I said, "Thank you," meaning it, and made way for him. I went home by tube, all the way this time, with my mind full of Claudio. I had been right about his appearance at least. He was no small, lithe man, and that was something gained. But he had frightened the woman at the Enquiries desk, and unlike Mr. Jessel, she would not frighten easily. As Peter had said, he was no good at not showing his feelings, and the feelings he had shown had frightened this enormously competent woman, enough to make her sink her professional dis-

cretion and warn me against him. I wondered, not for the
first time, but now with a very real disquiet, whether I had a
case of monomania on my hands. That, or something verging
on it, would explain as nothing else would the almost lunatic
persistence with which, after all these years, he was still following the thing up, and it would not be inconsistent with
the sort of character Peter had given him. His original resentment would have been against Peter himself, who he
would have felt had double-crossed him somehow and done
him out of his rights. Now there was only me. I imagined he
must have tried to put on some sort of act with the Enquiries
woman, no doubt turning on the charm which Peter said he
had, and which in a curious kind of way I still remembered.
But she had clearly disbelieved his act, which was no doubt
ineptly done because he was no good at them, and then he
had got angry. His anger, of course, would have been against
me, not her, and this she had been aware of. I did not like
the sound of it. He was a big man, all right, not a small one,
and he was no good at acts, but I was quite a bit afraid of
him, all the same.

But there was this much comfort in it. I now not only had
no compunction about killing him, I recognised it as an out-
right necessity. Whatever happened, and especially if I got
the thing we both wanted, I should never be safe as long as
he was alive. It was possible that Lisa Gaston might not be
either. I wondered for the first time whether she had thought
of that herself. I hoped not, but I wondered.

CHAPTER 8.

For some time after that I did nothing about Claudio except to beware of him. With any luck I had given him something to occupy his not over-bright mind and even perhaps his time. The idea that I might try to evade him by staying on the smaller island and making only day-trips, or single day-trip, to the one that mattered was one I thought might appeal to the cunning in him. It was the sort of over-elaborate plan, offering little real advantage to compensate for its over-elaboration, which a man of this type might think up for himself, and might therefore be ready to attribute to other people. I had to assume that he had had that amount of information from the Enquiries woman before she got suspicious of him and threw him out. I should have liked very much to ask her about this, but I did not want to involve her further, and I did not really think I should get anything more out of her if I tried. At least, if he had taken the bait, it would give him a reason for keeping me alive and for maintaining, and even tightening, his surveillance of my movements.

This brought in Mrs. Iacovou again, and any other local source of information he had or might try to acquire. I had gone to considerable lengths to try to patch up my relations with Mrs. Iacovou, greeting her when I saw her with the most innocent politeness, and gradually wooing her back, at least outwardly, to her old smiling friendliness, though I was conscious now of the inscrutability and cunning in the dark peasant's face, which made her, for all the differences between them, a sort of natural ally to Claudio. What I had said to her had been so vague that I hoped she could have persuaded herself that she had been mistaken in her understanding of it, and I wanted this for more than one reason. The first was the obvious one that, having identified her as Claudio's source of information, I was concerned that she should remain so, so that I should know where I was with her. Another was that if I could keep her in business, I might on occasion find her useful for feeding false information to the enemy. And lastly, I still could not help rather liking her and thought she probably needed the money, and it pleased me to think of her drawing it from Claudio's pocket for work which, now that I knew what she was up to, could only be of more use to me than to him. In any case, I thought it unlikely that she would have told him of my possible suspicion of her. I judged her a natural double-crosser, and the money, such as it was, was probably important to her. I reckoned she would go on giving him something for his money, even if she had to make it up, and it was to my advantage that she should believe what she gave him, and if necessary give him what I wanted him to have. But for some time after the Waterloo gambit I did not go out of my way to offer anything to either of them, and my real activities, whatever they made of them, were in fact of no significance whatever. I simply went back to my ordinary life and regular work.

This went on through the winter and well into the new year. I had another, more alarming, brush with Claudio later, when he was probably beginning to lose patience, but let that come in its proper place. The next thing that happened was totally unexpected and, in fact, changed the whole course of events. I had been asleep for a couple of hours one morning when I was awakened by a tapping on the door. I was out of bed and had the gun in my hand in very creditable time, but then I gave myself time to think. Whoever it was could not get in without breaking the door, and anyway if you intend frontal assault, you do not generally start by knocking politely for admission. What I had to fear was an attempt to get in by treachery or persuasion, but at the same time I badly needed to see who it was. To fling open the door with a gun in my hand, ready to shoot first, was fine so long as it was the enemy outside, but it might be an innocent neighbour or the management or even a policeman, and in none of those cases would it create a good impression. I decided on innocence with force in reserve. I put the light on because, for obvious reasons, the curtains were drawn and the room reasonably dark. Then I put on my dressing-gown. This may not seem to make much sense, but it is a fact that civilised man feels much less defenceless when he is reasonably fully clothed. Also, it was cold in the room, and cold slows down your reactions. Thus reinforced, I tiptoed over to the door and took up a position, not behind the swing of the door but against the wall next to its opening, with my gun pointing across the doorway, so that I could shoot or drop the gun into my dressing-gown pocket, as the situation required. Then I put my head close to the edge of the door, but not in any possible line of fire, and said, "Yes?"

It was a woman's voice that answered me. I could not identify it, not through the shut door, but I still had treachery in mind. It might even be Mrs. Iacovou, or some other female accomplice, with Claudio in the background ready to act if I opened the door incautiously. The voice said, "May I come in please?"

I stood back again, with the gun ready in my right hand, and with my left reached out and opened the latch-lock. Then I said, "Come in," and the door opened and Lisa Gaston came in. She walked into an apparently empty room, with a tousled but empty bed its most prominent object, and then turned and found herself looking into my gun, which I had been too startled to pocket. For a moment she stared at me with that suddenly remembered deadpan look, and then she smiled.

"Put that away, for God's sake," she said. "It frightens me."

I put it away, but not until I had shut the door and heard the latch-lock click home. Then I smiled back at her. I felt curiously empty and breathless. I said, "Lisa! What brings you here?"

She said, "I come to whet your almost blunted purpose," but she said it merely to answer my question, as if her mind was on something else. She looked at my dressing-gown and then turned and looked at the untidy bed behind her. "Why are you in bed?" she said. "Illness or idleness?" Again that terrible economy with words.

"Neither," I said. As before, I echoed her trick of speech. "I work nights and sleep days."

"As what?" she said.

"Night-watchman." But I found myself, disconcertedly, unwilling to leave her with the lantern-and-stick image. "They call it Night Security Officer," I said. "At a factory."

She nodded, and then a look of concern came over her face. It was not mere politeness, it was real concern. The dark eyes widened, and the mouth softened suddenly. It was there that her power lay, in the sheer feminine humanity under her incisiveness. "I'm sorry," she said. "I'd no idea. I've broken into your first sleep, and that's always the best."

"Don't worry," I said. I really wanted very badly to reassure her. "I don't sleep all day any more than you sleep all night. Only I'm sorry you find me in this disarray."

She looked me over, from my unkempt head to my bare feet. "You look very nice," she said. "Disarray suits you. A sweet disorder in the dress."

I thought, not only the Bard, the lyrists as well, but I had no reply to this. I merely shook my head at her. "Look," I said, "sit down, for God's sake, and I'll get the room warm and make some coffee for us." I pointed to my chair. I only had the one. When I had visitors, they spent most of their time on the bed, but I felt this explanation was beyond me.

She said, "All right," and sat down in my chair. It was a comfortable chair, and she made herself comfortable in it. It was too big for her, but she worked herself into it like a cat. I am fond of cats, and found this extraordinarily endearing. I lit the gas-stove, and dragged the clothes up over the bed, partly because it was untidy as it was, and partly because the open bed conveyed a suggestion that did not fit the relation between us. It was a big bed for a single man. I like a big bed, with or without visitors. Then I went to the stove and set about making coffee. I left it to her to do the talking. I thought she would not have come if she had not had something to say, but since I did not know what it was, I was not going to anticipate it. Meanwhile, she looked round the room, not critically, not in any way you could put a finger on at all, merely taking it all in. Finally she said, "So this is where you live."

"Where," I said, "and how." The kettle was on and the rest could wait. I turned and faced her.

She nodded. "I'm glad," she said. "I was right to come."

I said, "To whet my almost blunted purpose? That's not really fair, you know. Come to that, I've never thought the ghost was really fair to Hamlet. But then you can't expect ghosts to be fair minded. They must have a sense of grievance, or they wouldn't be ghosts."

"I have no sense of grievance," she said, "not against you, anyway, and I'm not a ghost. That wasn't really why I came."

I said, "I'm glad of that." Then I heard the kettle behind me dropping its voice to come to the boil, and I turned and saw to my coffee-making.

When she did speak, she had changed course again. She said, "What's been happening? Has Claudio showed himself?"

I had got so used to thinking of him as Claudio that I took her use of the name for granted. It was only later that it gave me food for thought. "Not fully," I said, "but he's around, all right. It's me he's been watching all this time, not Peter. He has a source of information two doors along the landing."

She nodded. "What do you mean, not fully?"

"I've seen his hands and his feet. I know he's a big man, and I suspect a flashy dresser. I also know that when he gets angry, he frightens people. He frightens me."

"But why?" she said. "I thought we'd agreed that you're safe from him for the present?"

"Two ways," I said. "First, he might try to nobble me and force the information out of me. If he had me well enough nobbled, he could get it, all right. I'm not that sort of a hero. What he'd do with me after he'd got it is anybody's guess, but I shouldn't fancy my chances. The other thing is that he may have an idea I'm after him—not only after whatever it is —and if he ever got to be as scared of me as I am of him, he might decide to cut his losses and get me first. But I don't think that's likely because I think he's got a fixation on the thing. He's been waiting for it all these years, and he's not going to give it up now, even at the risk of his own skin. He's an awkward customer, all right. But I still don't know who he is or where he lives, and I still can't remember him." I thought for a moment. "What about the police?" I said. "Is he in the clear so far as they are concerned? I've seen nothing about the case in the papers."

"So far as I know, they're at a dead end. You can't really blame them. He may not have been in the place more than an hour or two, and there's no known motive. They've had nothing from me, obviously. I'm not handing him over to the police, you know that. He'd go in for a few years and come out madder than ever. And in the meantime you and I would have been involved in all sorts of explanations we've no wish to give. And we can't shop him without explanations when we don't know who he is."

We had our coffee now, and for a moment or two she sipped hers, looking at me over her cup and saying nothing. Then she said, "If you did know who he was, would you consider shopping him? You could do it anonymously, and it would give you a clear run."

I shook my head, looking at her as straight as she was looking at me. "It wouldn't," I said. "If he was taken in, his one idea would be to stop me. He'd blow the whole thing sky-high, and what sort of a clear run should I get then? Besides, that wasn't the bargain, was it?"

"No," she said, but there was a touch of something like desolation in her voice. "No, that wasn't the bargain. But I have been wondering whether the bargain was a fair one. For you, I mean. At the time I felt—" She made a dismissive gesture with her hand and did not say what she had felt. "But I'm not sure I should have involved you in it. Or not on those terms."

80

"I could have refused it," I said. "I went into it with my eyes open."

"You need the money," she said. It was not a question now, it was a statement of fact. She had seen the way I lived, and knew I needed the money.

I said, "That's right, I need the money. Not immediately and desperately, but in the long run. I don't go hungry, and I don't get too bored, but I also don't see much of a future for myself. It's perfectly possible that this thing has no money in it at all. We've no idea what it is, or was. It may have ceased to exist, or it may have no negotiable value now. A special line in diamonds would no doubt be worth a lot more now than twenty years ago, only you don't pack diamonds in sealed steel boxes. Perishable is the last thing they are. But a piece of paper, say, could have been dynamite twenty years ago and be worthless now. Events can easily overtake pieces of paper. It's a gamble anyway. But as I stand, it's a gamble worth trying. And anyway, I'm stuck with the thing now. Not because of our bargain. Because of Claudio. He's not going to let it rest, even if I do. He's coming after me some time, whatever I do, and bargains apart I can see only one way of dealing with him."

She nodded. She was not looking at me now. She was staring into her empty coffee cup with that same visible concentration of thought I had seen in her before. I took her cup out of her hand and refilled it. She let it go almost without looking up. Only when I handed it back to her she raised her eyes and looked at me again. She said, "I was wondering, have you thought of reversing the roles?"

"Reversing them how?" I did not see what she meant at all.

"Well—letting him get hold of the information, or a version of it, and then going after him. You'd be on the offen-

sive then, and he'd be on the defensive, and that would suit
you better. But you'd have to know him first, I think, at least
by sight."

I smiled into her serious face. I could not help it. "What a
woman you are," I said. "I hadn't thought of that, and it's
clever. But it would mean total commitment on my part, because then the timing would be his. I'd have to leave my job,
almost for certain. It's not much of a job, but it's all I've got.
It would raise the stakes no end."

She said, "Well, I'll stake you. I might even help you play
your hand. It would be two to one then."

I had been perching on the edge of my half-made bed, but
now I got up and put my cup down by the stove and went
and stood over her as she sat in my chair looking up at me.
"But why, Lisa?" I said. "All these years you wouldn't let
Peter try his hand, let alone going in on it with him. And
now this? Why?"

She shook her head at me with a sort of gentle resignation,
so that I felt again, as I had felt with her once before, as if I
was a not very bright child who had to be made to understand. "I had Peter," she said. "I didn't want any change.
Now I've got nothing but a certain amount of money and a
house in Brancastle. You could say if you like I'm bored. It's
an understatement, but it's one way of putting it." There
was nothing gentle about her now. The eyes were narrowed
and the mouth drawn hard. This was the woman who had
told me to kill Claudio. She said, "I stopped Peter from going after the thing, but they killed him all the same. Now I'm
ready to go after it myself—it and Claudio. I handed the job
over to you, and I'm not taking it back. The bargain still
stands. But I'm ready to come in on your side if you'll have
me. I'm not without experience—I told you. I worked well

82

with Peter, and I expect I could work with you. And I want to see the thing finished."

For what seemed a very long time we stared at each other with nothing said. It was not a clash of wills. In a curious kind of way all contact between us had been broken, and I was considering her, and she me, both equally objectively. Then suddenly she smiled, and we were in contact again, but on an entirely different footing. I think these sudden, shattering changes in her were not so much changes of mood as changes of level. In herself she was all of a piece, but her mind seemed to work simultaneously on different levels, and she spoke sometimes out of one and sometimes out of another. As I say, the changes could be shattering, but she remained the same person. Now she said, "Look, you're missing your sleep, and I don't want that. You'd better go back to bed."

I said the only thing I knew for certain I meant. I said, "I don't want you to go."

She took this absolutely at its face value. "No?" she said. "Well, I needn't go yet. I've got nothing else to do. Can you sleep if I just sit here for a bit, or shall I stop you sleeping?"

"You won't stop me sleeping," I said, and knew it was true. To sleep with her sitting quietly beside me seemed to me the perfect way of arranging things.

She nodded. "All right," she said. "Into bed with you, then."

I stood back from her and took off my dressing-gown, gun and all, and got into bed. When I had settled myself, I said, "You might say, 'Sleep thou, and I will wind thee in my arms,'" but she laughed and shook her head.

"You have to remember who that was said to," she said. "Bottom the weaver. A skilled mechanic with a yen for prominence, and an ass's head to boot. God's own shop-steward born before his time."

I said, "By my faith, she is very swift and sententious." I left her to work on that one, and turned my back on her and settled myself to go to sleep. Sleep would come easily enough. I had not felt such peace for God knows how many uneasy years.

It was past midday when I woke. I drifted awake gradually, conscious of a sense of peace before I remembered the reason for it. When I did remember, I lay very still, because there was a weight of warmth and softness on the bed beside me. Not in the bed, obviously, but on it, so that I felt the warmth and the downward drag of the bedclothes on my body. I lay still, letting the consciousness wrap my wind, but my breathing must have changed, because there was a sudden gentle movement on the bed beside me, and when I let myself open my eyes and turn round, she was in the chair, where I had last seen her, but with her head down and her eyes shut. I put a hand out and felt the warmth on the coverlet. It was real warmth and very localised. I said, "Lisa" very quietly, and she lifted her head and opened her eyes and looked at me. For the first time since I had known her, there was a touch of colour in the pale face.

"I've been asleep," she said.

I said, "Yes, Lisa, you've been asleep. So have I. I feel much better for it. I hope you do."

She said, "Yes, thank you," but the colour had gone now, and she was as cool as a cucumber. There was no shaking her out of her composure, and in any case I did not want to. She looked at her watch. "I must be going," she said. "There's a train I can catch."

I got out of bed and put on my dressing-gown, with the gun still bumping against my leg as I pulled it round me. I

84

asked the question I should have asked before. I said, "Do you suppose Claudio knows you by sight?"

She answered without hesitation. She had clearly been over the ground already. "I think almost certainly not," she said. "I think probably he simply followed you up to the cottage, or near it, and then lay up somewhere waiting for dusk. Then I think he must have taken up a position near the path. It would have given him a shock seeing what he thought was you coming up the path, not down it, but in any case he did what he had come to do. Then I think he shifted Peter's body to where he hoped it wouldn't be found, and got the hell out. He must have known his mistake by then, but there was nothing else he could do. He didn't want both of you dead. You were his one chance now. All he could do was to go back to watching you. In any case, he wouldn't have hung about at Brancastle, not once he had killed Peter. I don't think he can have seen me at all. You didn't see me until the funeral, and he'd have been long gone by then. And in any case, why should he want to?"

I nodded a little reluctantly. "I hope you're right," I said. "I think you probably are, and I certainly hope so."

She got up out of my chair. "Then I've done no harm coming, and shall do no harm going," she said. "I might have been visiting anyone in the building. So long as I'm not seen leaving your room. I wasn't seen coming in."

I did not think, in fact, that even that would do any harm. Mrs. Iacovou might note an unusual face, but would assume the usual explanation. But I was not going to explain that to Lisa, not now of all times. I said, "The building won't be watched now. I'm supposed to be asleep. As for this room, I'll see it's clear to the head of the stairs, and after that, as you say, you might have been visiting anyone."

She nodded. "Very well. Then I'll go now."

85

I said, "I haven't given you an answer."

"I haven't asked for one," she said. "It's not a question of yes or no. Think the whole thing over in view of what I've said, and tell me what you think should be done. But we've got to know what he looks like. Until we do, we're fighting blindfold."

"All right," I said, "I agree. What shall I do? Write?"

"I don't see why not. It's not the police we're up against. But remember the name's Mowbray. Now see me out, will you?"

I went to the door and opened it cautiously. There was no one on the landing, and the other doors were shut. "All clear," I said. "Good-bye, Lisa. Thank you for coming."

"I had to," she said. There was a world of meaning in the words, but nothing for me personally. "Good-bye, then, Ben." She stopped and looked at me for a moment. "What's Ben short for?" she said. "Benjamin?"

"That's right."

"Not Benedick?"

"Not Benedick, no."

"A pity," she said. "I'd have liked that."

Then she was gone. We did not even touch hands. I watched her to the head of the stairs, and then went in and shut the door.

CHAPTER 9.

I wrote to Lisa Gaston about a week later. It was a strictly business letter—at least to start with. I thought that if we ever came to be on other than strictly business terms, it would be for her to dictate them, not me. I wrote: "I am going to make a deliberate attempt at a sighting. If it doesn't come off, I think I'll ask you to come down and help. It should be easy enough for you to get one, using me as bait, always providing you are not already identified. You might even get an address. Anyway, let me have a try first. You will see from this that I am not by any means rejecting your suggestion. But on all accounts, and on all possible assumptions, the longer you keep out of it, the more decisive your intervention is likely to be." At the end I weakened. I did not want her to think that the strictly business tone was of my choosing. I added: "In any case, thank you very much for coming down. At the moment I think we have a pretty sad and nasty business on our hands, but, one way or another, it can't last for ever, and hereafter, as Le Beau says to Orlando (very much as one gentleman to another), hereafter in a better world than this I shall desire more love and knowledge of you."

I posted the letter on my way to work, and set about priming Mrs. Iacovou. I knew near enough when she went out to do her shopping, even though it was when I was generally asleep. It would need no more than some slight sacrifice of sleep to contrive to meet her on the stairs. Or better still, I thought, to be close on her heels when she started up them on her return. She climbed them very slowly, panting a bit over her laden bag, and if I offered to carry it for her, it would give me a lead in, and I should have three flights, taken at her pace, to get my message across. This meant some hanging about, and a little mild scouting, but at the third attempt I got the timing right. She had paused in the hall and put her bag down beside her, and stood there, looking with a sort of stoical resignation at the stairs ahead. Why she did not use the lift I had no idea, but she was probably afraid of it, even if she knew how to work it, which was doubtful. I said, "Good-morning, Mrs. Iacovou. Going up? Let me carry that bag for you. It looks heavy."

She turned, as deliberately as she did everything, and said, "Good-morning, Mr. Selby." She gave me her usual wide smile. She seemed still to have a complete set of teeth, inevitably a bit yellowed with age, but very striking in that brown, wizened face. The smile involved her whole face, activating a completely fresh system of wrinkles in the parchment skin, but did not seem, now that I knew her better, to include the eyes, which remained opaque and calculating. For what seemed quite a time the face smiled at me and the eyes considered me, so that I began to have doubts about the success of my efforts to disarm her. But whatever she thought, she had no good reason to refuse my offer, and the bag remained heavy and the stairs high. She said, "Thank you. You are very kind. But I go very slowly."

I stooped and picked up the bag. It was, in fact, surprisingly heavy, and I wondered how far she had had to carry it already. I thought that probably, like many tough old people, she had strong muscles but was getting short of wind. At her own pace she could manage the flat streets, but the stairs

taxed her. I weighed the bag in my hand, full of an exagger-
ated surprise and concern. I said, "My goodness, it's heavy.
You must be very strong." I was all breezy geniality.

She said, "I am strong, thank God," and we started up the
stairs.

"You go ahead," I said. "And go as slow as you like. I'm in
no hurry."

She nodded and began climbing, and I followed a couple
of steps behind her. It was at the top of the first flight that
she paused and asked her first question. It was not put like a
question. None of her questions were. I suppose it was something to do with her native tongue. She used only the gram-
matical affirmative. You recognised the question only by the
tone of her voice or by the conversational context, and it was
not difficult to miss it altogether. Now she said, "You have
not gone to bed yet."

I had not, in fact, come prepared with an explanation, and
I used the opportunity to turn the conversation the way I
wanted. I said, "The truth is, I like to get a little sunlight,
now that the days are longer." Whatever this was, it was not
the truth. I did not give a damn about the sunlight. But at
least it made it just possible to add, "Still, I'm hoping to get
a couple of days off next week."

She had started up the next flight of stairs, but now she
stopped, three stairs up, and turned to face me. I was already on the bottom stair, but even so our heads were almost
on a level. The risers of the steep concrete stairs were a good
seven inches high, and for all her stocky peasant build she
was no dwarf. The mental effect was very striking. I had always hitherto seen Mrs. Iacovou from on top, but now she
looked at me, not up from under her heavy brows, but eyeball to eyeball and from slightly above me. I thought how

frightening she would be, if she wanted to, to her children and grandchildren. She said, "You are going away?"

This was the question I had wanted her to ask, but it was very direct and slightly unnerving. I had not said anything about going away, only about taking a few days off work, but it was my going away she was interested in. I said, "I'm thinking of it, yes. A couple of days in the sun would be nice."

She nodded. She said, "You will go far next week?" Even the timing she wanted to be sure of. There was plenty of cunning in her, but not much subtlety. Claudio all over again.

I smiled at her pleasantly and a little vaguely. I think I even shrugged slightly. "I don't know," I said. "Not too far, I should think. But out of London, anyway."

She stared at me impenetrably for a moment, but did not venture on any further question. Instead she nodded again. "That is good," she said, and went on up the stairs. She went up them steadily, breathing heavily as I had expected but keeping on at it, and I went after her with that damned heavy bag, a little breathless myself, and not only for physical reasons. I had stopped liking Mrs. Iacovou. I should not have minded if she had dropped dead under my feet, except that I wanted her to relay my misinformation to Claudio. She did not drop dead, of course. She got to her door and stopped and turned and put out a brown leathery hand for the bag. We were on level ground now, and she was looking up at me again. The wrinkles re-arranged themselves, and she gave me her flashing smile, with her eyes still watching me, just as she had downstairs. She said again, "Thank you, Mr. Selby. You are very kind."

I said, "Not a bit, Mrs. Iacovou. It was a pleasure." It had been, too, but not in the way I said it. I went off along the landing towards my door. "And to hell with you, Mrs. Iacovou," I said, but I did not say it aloud. I waited for her door to shut behind me before I opened mine. For all I knew, she had already seen the second lock, but in case she had not, I did not want to draw attention to it.

I did not, in fact, take any time off the following week. All I did was to give up the best part of a day's sleep, but I could still do that without undue loss of efficiency, provided I did not do it too often. On the Tuesday I contrived a meeting with Mrs. Iacovou and told her I was off next day, though I remained vague about details. I wanted to make it as easy for the enemy as possible without throwing the thing too much in their faces. To do Claudio justice, I thought he must have suspected something if he had known the details of my dealing with Mrs. Iacovou, but I did not think he would. Even if she still suspected something herself, as she well might, I trusted her to be sufficiently untrustworthy to conceal her doubts from Claudio. I reckoned I had a divided opposition to deal with, and dealt with it accordingly.

On Wednesday morning I walked out of the building and took the tube to Waterloo. I carried what might be taken for a week-end case, though it was packed with nothing but a couple of spare blankets. I had to pack it with something, because you handle an empty case quite differently from a full one, and that was the sort of thing Claudio might notice, but I was not going to disturb my possessions by packing the things I should have packed if I had been going where I was supposed to be going. I had picked a train going the same way as the island boat-train, but leaving before the boat-train itself, so that I could, if I had wanted, have left my train and joined the boat-train further down the line. I did not, of course, want to do anything of the sort, but I thought

91

that that was just the sort of elementary deviousness which Claudio would expect of me.

I got to Waterloo with no evidence that I was being followed, but then I had not looked for any. I joined a fair-sized queue at the booking office, and without any too obvious looking over my shoulder felt it filling up comfortably behind me as I shuffled forward towards the ticket window. I did not think Claudio would try fishing for information about my booking in any case, not after the rebuff he seemed to have had at the enquiry office, but I wanted to make it as difficult for him as possible in case he did try. When I got to the window, I took a single to the first station the train stopped at, which was a junction hardly clear of the suburbs. This was mainly meanness on my part. I had to go through the motions of buying a ticket, and I had to have a ticket which would admit me without explanations to the platform the train was leaving from. Subject to that, I just wanted to do the thing as cheaply as possible. I did not intend, if I could help it, to travel even that far, and I rational-ised my meanness by arguing that, even if Claudio managed somehow to find out where I was booked to, he would ac-cept it as part of the process of covering my tracks. I did not so much as look at the queue when I left the ticket window. Wherever he was and whatever he was up to, I did not sup-pose Claudio would buy a ticket himself until he saw what train I was going on, and I had given him plenty of time for that. My train was in fact already at the platform, but it was not due to leave for nearly half an hour yet. I walked casu-ally to a bookstall and bought myself a paper. Then I went to the barrier, showed my ticket and walked out along the plat-form towards the front of the train.

It was suddenly curiously quiet after the bustle of the public part of the station, what they now call the concourse.

I have noticed that before at stations, especially London ter-
mini. One moment you are part of the London crowds, and
the next, by virtue of your ticket, you are a privileged occupant of private ground, and if you are early enough, or the
train is not a busy one, the ground can be very private indeed. I walked steadily along the platform, with the noise of
the station dying away behind me, an empty bay on my left
and the empty train standing silent and deserted on my
right. There are few things more oppressively empty than an
empty train. I went on down the long line of windows, peering in through the glass at the dusky rows of seats. The windows and doors were all tight shut. It is the cleaners who do
this, sealing the train coach by coach as they finish cleaning
it, I suppose so that no dust can get in and spoil their handi-
work. The fact that the air could do with changing is no concern of theirs.

There was no engine on the train yet, just the leading
coach standing with its nose almost in the sunlight, waiting
for the engine to back onto it. There was no one about at all.
My plan was a very simple one. I was going to walk most of
the way out along the platform and get in near the front of
the train. Then instead of settling into a seat, I was going to
double back as fast as I could without leaving the train, and
take up a position in the rear coach, near but not too near a
window overlooking the platform. I reckoned Claudio would
see me well along the platform and probably actually into
the train. Then he would buy himself a ticket and come
along after me. He would wait, probably, until there was a
fair stream of passengers joining the train and then come
along with them. He would locate me, and find himself a
seat near enough to be sure he would see me if I made any
move to leave the train. This was all routine stuff. Only by
the time he got back with his ticket, I should be, not where

93

he had last seen me at the front of the train, but back at the rear, with a good view of him as he came along the platform. Once I had had my sight of him and given him time to get well along the platform, I could simply get out, go out through the barrier on some pretext and find my way home. How long it would take him to make up his mind that he had lost me I had no idea, but I liked to think he would have to commit himself to the journey and go along with the train before he could be sure.

I had reached about the third coach from the front when I suddenly knew, just as I had that day in the tube train, that the hunt was on. It is difficult to say exactly what the feeling consists of. If I had to locate it anywhere, I should say the back of the neck, whether because it is a hotchpot of nervous cords anyway, or because from the time he first got up on his back legs man must have known that if he was attacked from behind, that was his weak spot. But whatever it is and wherever it hits you, the thing is a kind of fear, and I was doubly disturbed, by the fear itself and by the fact that I was feeling it now. If Claudio was there, and I had no doubt he was, I ought to have been pleased. I had done all I could to get him to come along, and up to now I had had no awareness of his presence, any more than I had when I had taken him to the enquiries office several months back. Yet here, out at the end of the empty platform, with the empty train beside me, I was suddenly and simultaneously aware that I was being watched and afraid of the watcher. I told myself that it was the unexpected and somehow unnatural solitude that had laid me open to it. I reminded myself that in any case I was the hunter and not the hunted. I still did not like the feeling any better.

I turned sharp to the right and put my hand on the handle of the first carriage door I came to. It was a corridor-coach of the old type, not one of the new open-plan ones, and the corridor was on my side. Beyond it I could see into a single shadowy compartment, standing as empty and silent as a robbed tomb, but from where I was I could see no more than a corner of each of its neighbours, and nothing at all of the other compartments along the coach. I had a sudden picture of a very large figure, standing somewhere in the coach where I could not see it, waiting with a knife in its hand. But I knew this was nonsense. I pulled down the handle, swung the door open and stepped into the stuffy air of the corridor. There was a faint smell of smoke in the air. It is curious, after all these years of diesel and electric traction, how some railway coaches still seem to smell of the age of steam. I supposed it was really stale tobacco smoke, but the compartments at hand were non-smokers, and I wondered who had been smoking here and how long since. The cleaners, I thought. Half the cleaning women I had ever seen seemed to do their work with a cigarette in their mouth, and this lot had finished their work, and shut the coach up tight, and left the smell of their smoke behind them. There was nothing to worry about, anyway. Claudio was away on the far side of the barrier buying himself a ticket, and I must get back to the rear of the train and find my vantage point before he returned to the barrier, and showed his ticket at the gate, and came walking in full view along the platform. I shut the door with a crash behind me, took my case of blankets in my left hand and started back along the corridor.

The boat-train would no doubt have been all new rolling-stock, but this was a stopping train with few pretensions, and the coaches were a mixture of old and not-so-old. From the end of the corridor I emerged into an open-plan coach, and from that into another. There was more window space here, but there still seemed to be nobody about on the platform. Then I was in a corridor again, making my way, as one does, half sideways, with the case in my left hand occasionally bumping the backs of my knees. I was in a hurry, consciously because I wanted to get well into position before Claudio came back along the platform, but also I believe because of an unacknowledged urge to get back as quickly as possible to the more populated part of the station.

What would have resulted if it had been an open-plan coach I shall never know, but it was in a corridor coach that the thing happened. It happened just as I came into the front end of the coach. I had come through the canvas concertina giving access from the coach ahead and was in the end space of the coach, with a carriage door on one side and a lavatory tucked into one corner. It was the space where, in the old days of crowded trains, you used to dump your suitcase and sit on it when there was no proper seat available. Going as I was, leaning forward and as it were headfirst, I had my head into the end of the corridor before much of the rest of me negotiated the corner, and that was as far as I got. There was a very large man filling the other end of the corridor.

He must have come into the rear end of the coach a moment before I came into the front, because he was clear into the corridor before my head came round the corner. He was not looking in my direction, but moving with his head turned sideways, looking into the compartments on his right as he came towards me. I could not see his face, only an expanse of red neck between the dark brown of his jacket and the beige-brown of his felt hat. I whipped back round the corner as his head was turning again, and my case bumped once, not very loudly, on the wooden panelling behind me. I could not know whether he had heard the bump, but in any case there was no time to think about it. It was no use going

96

back the way I had come. Even if I could keep ahead of him, which was doubtful with a case in my hand, he would only be driving me into a corner at the deserted end of the platform, and I did not at all fancy that. I thought for a moment of opening a door on the far side of the train and climbing down onto the rails of the next track, but even as I considered it the thing was decided for me. Suddenly, but with a sort of inexorable slowness, another train slid past the windows to take up its position against the far platform. If it had been full of passengers, there might have been hope in it, but compartment after compartment slid by me with no one in them. The train was as empty as mine. By now I was through the concertina and into the end space of the next coach. I could not hear anyone moving, but I knew that almost in a matter of seconds he would emerge out of the concertina, and we should be face to face. I opened the door of the lavatory, got myself and my case inside, all as quietly as possible, and shut and locked the door behind me. Then I stood and waited.

I was angry now as well as frightened. I was angry because I had underestimated the enemy. At the best I had underestimated him. At the worst, and it was very much worse, I had mistaken his intentions altogether. The one thing I had been certain of in my split-second view of him was that he was not carrying a case. Unless he had dumped it somewhere at the rear end of the train, it looked as if he was not proposing to travel at all, and if that was so, I could only wonder what it was he had in mind to do when he caught up with me. I was also very angry at the sheer silliness of my position. Not only was I the hunted instead of the hunter, I was the hunted gone to earth in a second-class lavatory compartment, with a small window of frosted glass at my back and a door in front fastened by a single brass bolt which, merely by being shot, proclaimed to anyone outside that the lavatory was occupied. I did not know what Claudio would do. I thought a lot depended on whether he had heard my case bump the panelling as I had whisked back round the corner, and if so what he had made of it. I was confident that he had not seen me, but he might have heard someone. Even if he had, I did not think he could be certain it was me, because I did not think he could be certain that no one else had got into the train after I had. Whatever his intentions, and however quickly he had acted, he must have had to get a ticket of some sort to get through the barrier, and even a platform ticket takes longer to acquire than it did. If he was merely looking for me as an unsuspecting passenger on the train, I could not believe that he would check all the lavatories as he worked his way towards the front, at least not the first time. Of all things, I took curious comfort in the ancient, almost ritual, prohibition against using the lavatory while the train was in a station. We have all grown up with it. I remember once hearing it expanded into an elegant lyric and sung to a popular air. No one, I argued, or at least no one with any sense of the fitness of things, was going to board a train, especially at a London terminus, and immediately, in defiance of all the established proprieties, repair to the lavatory. Especially, I thought, taking his suitcase with him, and Claudio would know I had one. If he had found my suitcase in a compartment and no sign of me, the lavatory might well be the first thing he thought of, but he had so far seen nothing of me on the train at all, and so far as he knew, I was still up near the front end where he had seen me get aboard. He had, it was true, surprised me by deciding to search for me systematically from the rear coach forward, but his search had so far yielded nothing to set him checking the lavatories. Unless, I thought, he happened to see the Engaged sign on the lavatory door as he went past. I decided to draw the bolt back to read Vacant on the outside, but to keep a hand ready to shoot it home if anyone tried the door. I still think, despite the total ridiculousness of my position, it was a brave decision to make, but I had no time to carry it out. As I put my hand to the bolt, I heard footsteps come through the concertina and into the space outside the door, and then it was too late. A lavatory door which said Engaged might be easy to miss as you went past, but a door which changed from Engaged to Vacant in front of your eyes invited curiosity, and if it then failed to disgorge its occupant would be downright suspicious.

I stood there, with my case end-up on the seat behind me and my hand outstretched to the bolt of the door, and knew, almost at once, that whoever it was outside was standing still too. The heavy footsteps had not, as I had hoped, passed without stopping. They had stopped without passing. I thought, or perhaps imagined, that I could hear breathing on the other side of the door, but I could hear no movement at all. Very carefully my right hand came back from the door and reached under the bottom of my jacket to behind my right hip. As the long blade slid out of its sheath, the handle of the door, gently and in total silence, moved down, and paused for a moment, and moved up again. I tried to decide, if he kicked the door in, what would be the best way of dealing with him in the confined space available.

Whether, left to himself, he really would have kicked the door in I do not know. To kick it in on an innocent and unknown occupant would have been to invite very serious trouble indeed, and he still could not be sure that I was not further up the train. But he was not left to himself. Relief arrived inevitably but at the last possible moment, like the sheriff's posse. Someone swung the carriage door open on

the side next to the platform, and there was a babel of voices
and the noises of what sounded like a large family party getting its baggage aboard. Claudio would have to move. A man
of that size obstructs any passage, and, whatever size you
are, you cannot be seen mounting guard indefinitely over an
occupied lavatory compartment, at least not when the train
is at a platform and virtually every other lavatory on it is vacant and at your disposal. There was only one thing for him
to do. He had to complete his sweep of the train. If he found
me nowhere else, he could always return to his present
watch. But he still, after all, had no reason to suppose that I
knew he was on the train, or indeed following me at all. I
might on principle be covering my tracks, even to the extent
of locking myself in the lavatory until the train started, but
there was no apparent reason why I should not go on with
my journey, and indeed he presumably wanted me to go on
with it, so long as he did not lose track of me on the way.

In the general confusion I did not hear him go, but the
folk movement on the other side of the door was in full
swing now, and I could not believe there was room for him
as well. Moreover, they were moving themselves forward,
into one of the rear compartments of the coach, and if as I
supposed he had gone forward to continue his search, they
would now be between me and him. I put the knife away,
took my case in my left hand and with my right cautiously
slid back the bolt and turned the handle of the door. It
opened immediately from the pressure of a body against it,
but it was the back of a body, and a female one at that, un-
wisely but invitingly dressed in tight bell-bottomed trousers.
I swung the door back and stepped into the breach, deliberately adding to the confusion by colliding firmly with the en-
croaching softness. There was a startled squawk and giggled
apologies, but I was concerned neither with the social em-

barrassment nor with the potential pleasure of the encounter. I was looking for Claudio, but he was nowhere to be seen. I had to gamble on his having gone forward, and I forced my way, with muttered apologies but complete ruthlessness, through the encumbering bodies towards the concertina and the rear of the train.

There were people getting in all along the train now, and more on the platform. I was at least safe from attack, and for the rest, while I still hoped to get through the barrier without Claudio's seeing me, I was prepared to yield the moral victory to him. I had not seen his face, but I reckoned I had seen enough of him now to recognise him again in most circumstances. I still did not know who he was, but I was not, at the moment, staying to find out.

I fought my way down the train for another couple of coaches and then gave it up and got out onto the platform. I was still swimming against the tide, but there was more room here. At the barrier the man cocked an eye at me, and I waved my ticket at him. "Got to telephone," I said, and he nodded. It was his job to see that no one got onto the platform without a ticket, not that no one left with one.

"Better make it snappy," he said. "She goes in ten minutes." I nodded back and made for the taxis. I was back on course now, a bit ruffled, but doing what I had planned to do and seeing my way ahead. I got to my room unseen and as far as I could tell unheard, locked myself in, put my case of blankets in a corner, drew the curtains close, undressed and got into bed. I was tired now, and got to sleep almost at once.

It was several hours before I woke, and I woke then only because someone was tapping at my door. It was a very gentle, surreptitious tapping, as if whoever it was wanted to be heard inside the room but not outside in the corridor. I turned my head, very cautiously, to watch the door, but otherwise did not move. The tapping was repeated twice, and then whoever it was gave it up. They must have gone away, but I did not hear them go. Mrs. Iacovou, I thought. Claudio had lost me and wanted to know if I had gone home. That probably meant that he had not gone off on the train, and I wondered what he had told the man at the barrier. Or perhaps, like me, he had booked only to the first stop, and had got off when he was satisfied, lavatories and all, that I was not on the train. I reckoned he could have done that and still been back in London in time to alert Mrs. Iacovou. Now with any luck she would signal a negative, and then he would not know where I was, which was satisfactory as far as it went. I was sorry he had not gone all the way on the train, but I was not going to let regret keep me awake. I turned over, still very quietly, and went to sleep again.

CHAPTER 10.

I do not know how long it was before Mrs. Iacovou knew for certain I was home again. She must have known by the week-end, or at any rate Claudio must have, to do what he did. He must also have been a bit desperate, or very angry, or perhaps a bit of both. He was probably still uncertain what had happened to me after he had lost me at Waterloo, and may even have had a wild apprehension of my having after all got to the island without him. I do not know, because one way and another we never gave ourselves time to discuss the matter.

On the Sunday afternoon I went for my weekly walk on Wimbledon Common. For anyone living where I did, it was much the nearest place where you could still, if you picked your way and did not look about you too often, go quite a distance without actually seeing houses. Also it has, at least for me, a curious fascination of its own. All heathlands give me the creeps a bit. I think that is because they are intrinsically hostile to man as he now is, and yet for unimaginably long ages must have been the only sort of country man could live in as he then was. It is a bit like visiting the labourer's cottage or slum tenement where your grandfather grew up, and trying not to remember how very much like you he must, in fact, have been, even in a place like this. A bit of still recognisable heathland stuck in the middle of one of the plusher inner suburbs is a place where anything could hap-

pen, and I suspect does, especially after dark, when the
week-end riders and red-jacketed golfers and family dog-
walkers have got off back under their roofs, and the wind on
the heath, brother, is a lot colder than it was. I suppose that
is how the Wombles have made all their money, but it is not
really Wombles I have in mind.

Nothing happened to me, in fact, on Wimbledon Common, and I had no apprehension of mischief at any point of
my walk, though it was a grey day with not many people
about, and most of the time I was very much on my own.
When I got back to the car, which I had left parked with
others on one of the crossing roads, that too was on its own.
I saw with surprise that the locking nob of the door was up,
though I thought I had locked the door before I left. Even
this did not alert me, and I had settled myself in the driving
seat before I felt there was anything wrong. By then it was
too late. The bag was over my head and shoulders before I
heard any movement behind me, and my hands were still on
the wheel when a pair of arms like boa-constrictors dragged
the bag down to my hips. It whipped my arms to my sides
and pinned them there, and a moment later a running noose
was dropped over the whole bundle and jerked wickedly
tight at a point just above my elbows. It was a very neat professional job, perhaps unnecessarily violent, but then I
should have known better than to make Claudio angry. At
least I knew enough not to make any attempt at resistance.
Above all I knew that, although I was blindfold and would
shortly be gagged, I was not going to be suffocated. The bag
would have plenty of air-vents, though not where I could see
them. It is important to know this, because panic and claus-
trophobia can play hell with the heart and respiration, and a
fair number of deaths from suffocation are largely self-in-
duced. Angry or not, he never said anything, but worked

with a silent efficiency I found far from reassuring. I myself said nothing either, at first because there was nothing I wanted to say and then because I was physically prevented. He dragged me bodily out of the driver's seat and onto the back seat beside him, pushing me down to the floor, and even pulling the bag clear of the upper part of my face, to make sure I had enough air to breathe if I did not rush it. Finally he tied my ankles, using what felt like a webbing strap, pulled tight enough in all conscience, but less likely than a cord would have been to stop the circulation. For the moment all these considerations made life easier, but I did not like the implications. I thought he wanted me in fair physical shape, ready, so to speak, for immediate use when he had me wherever he was taking me. When he had finished, he did not get out of the car, because I heard no door opened or shut. He must have slithered over into the driving seat just as he had dragged me out of it, which for a man of his size and weight represented a fair piece of agility. All I heard was a certain amount of muffled movement, and the next moment the engine started and we were off.

He drove as fast as he could without attracting unwanted attention, and very smoothly. Whatever I thought of his intelligence, there was no denying his physical efficiency. I found it difficult to say how long we drove, but after a bit the speed picked up to such an extent that I knew we must be heading out of town on one of the motorways. I should like to be able to say that I considered the situation sensibly and laid plans for dealing with what lay ahead, but the truth is that my mind was very largely a blank, and I think I even made a conscious effort to keep it so. I was so completely in Claudio's power that the next move must in any case lie with him, and I could only deal with it when it came. In the meantime my paramount instinct was to conserve my energy—nervous, physical, even, if you like, mental. It must be with the same sort of instinct that the weaker creature, once caught, lies totally inert in the grip of the predator, I suppose ready for a last convulsive effort to escape if the chance ever comes. At some point the car lost speed, climbed a short distance and then swung round what must be a roundabout, and I knew we were off the motorway. Even allowing for motorway speeds, I did not think we could have come very far, forty or fifty miles perhaps at the most. I did not know in which direction, but it was unlikely to be south. I thought we had come too far for that, and had taken too long to get out of London. On the whole I settled for one of the inner shires, north or west. I did not really think it mattered, but perhaps took comfort from being even that far in mental control of the situation.

The speed was dropping now all the time, and there was a lot of gear-changing and sharp but always cautious cornering, which suggested country lanes. It must be nearly dark, but I fancied Claudio would put off using his lights as long as he could. Lights show a long way off in relatively flat country, and country people have in general a fair idea what cars may be expected where, especially on a Sunday evening. The journey did not, in fact, last much longer. The car suddenly slowed to a crawl, swung very sharp left and began lurching steeply uphill over very bad going. I had a picture of a rutted track, used if at all only by tractors, leaving the tarmac lane and climbing a small hill to some sort of pre-selected hide-out at the top. An isolated barn, perhaps, or a derelict cottage, even a spinny of trees if the covert was thick enough. Then the car crawled onto level ground and stopped.

For a moment or two there was complete silence. I expect Claudio was having a look round before he so much as got out of the car. Then the driver's door opened and shut, and the door next to me opened. There was another silence. He was probably waiting for me to do something, and then, when I did not, checking my breathing to make sure I was still with him. I went on doing nothing, and after a bit he reached in and undid the strap or whatever it was round my ankles. Then for the first time I heard his voice. "Out," he said.

It was a less deep and powerful voice than you would expect from a man of that physique, and thanks to the mystery of the English dipthong even that monosyllable told me something. I could swear it was a West Country voice, and for some reason I found that comforting. God knows the West Country has produced some tough characters in its time, but to my mind at least it remains indefeasibly free of the taint of real urban wickedness. I offer no logical defence for my feeling. I can only say that once I identified Claudio as a West Countryman, I felt less afraid of him. Also, I think, that curiously light voice in that massive body suggested a touch of physically-rooted immaturity. A man who looked like that but spoke like that might indeed be the sort of man who would build up a largely imaginary grievance into a murderous monomania. I am not saying that I worked all this out in the split second after he spoke. But I was certainly immediately conscious of a sense of relief, and I think, looking back, that this was what it was based on. Meanwhile, it was the monomania I had to deal with, not the man, and when he said, "Out," out I got.

My legs were no worse than a bit stiff, but I made a clumsy business of it, bundled up like that. If you think I am complaining unduly, I can only suggest you try some time getting out of the back seat of a car with your arms held close to your sides. He laid a massive grip on my left upper arm and piloted me a short distance over rather difficult going. The ground was level enough, and so hard it could almost be paved, but there were small, unexpected obstacles in the way of blind feet. Even before I got the smell through the air-holes of the bag, I was fairly certain that it was a building of some sort we had come to, probably a derelict building with bits of loose rubble or fallen roofing lying round it, and the smell, when I did get it, was unmistakable. Claudio's hide-out was a ruinous building of some sort standing at the top of a small but steep rise above the level of the surrounding lanes. Unless there was thick greenery round it, I thought the car would almost certainly be visible from some way off, and this turned out to be not only true, but the decisive factor in what followed.

He opened a door which groaned on its hinges like something in a radio play. It is curious how sounds ham it up when the other senses are temporarily out of action. I should not have been surprised if at any moment the wind had moaned in the chimney or an owl hooted in the dusk. I do not believe for a moment that the permanently impaired, the blind or the deaf, really develop extra capability in the remaining senses, as they are said to do, but they must attach enormously increased importance to what they do perceive and out of necessity grow better at interpreting it. If I went back there today, which I have no wish to do, I should probably hardly hear the door complain when I pushed it open, or notice except in passing the smell of damp stone and rotten woodwork which during most of the time I was there made up my whole knowledge of the place.

Claudio steered me in through the open door, and I went unresisting. He did not push the conventional gun into the small of my back, nor did I for a moment contemplate any sort of resistance. We both knew the odds too well for that.

108

We went a few more paces forward, and then he turned me round and backed me up against something straight and hard which took me vertically between the shoulder blades. It felt like a wooden post, and I found later that it was the stud of an internal partition wall from which the masonry or plaster had fallen away. Before I was well aware of it, his great arms whipped round me and added another couple of turns of rope to the standing cocoon, this time including the post. I made the gesture of trying to hold myself a little clear of the post to leave potential slack in the rope, but he would have none of it. He put one hand on my chest and forced me back against it while the other hand took the strain, and when he had finished, the rope was rigid round me and the post hard against my shoulders. Then and only then he put his hands behind my head and took off the gag. Then he stood away from me, and once more there was one of those total silences in which nothing moved but someone might at any moment speak.

This time he did. He said, "How's it feel?"

I worked my mouth into usable shape and said, "My arms. They're dead from the elbows down."

He pushed a knowledgeable finger under the rope that held my arms to my sides. It was exactly like a groom feeling the tightness of the girth against a horse's ribs. "They're not," he said. It was true, of course, but you have to try. Once more he stood back from me, because when he spoke again, his voice came from further off, in the direction of the door. He said, "I'll give you half-an-hour to think about it. You know what I want from you, and you know I'll get it. What happens first is up to you. You know about that, too. You think it over." He paused. "And don't try pulling at the post," he said. "You won't move it, and if you did, ten to one you'd have the roof on top of you, from what it looks like."

Then the door groaned again, and a moment or two later I heard the car start. It started and manoeuvred a bit, and then went off away from me down the track. I had been right about one thing at least. The car was too noticeable and too inexplicable where it was, and he had to put it somewhere else or risk being interrupted. With all that, giving me time to think was not bad practice either, and often saves all parties a great deal of trouble. I did not see Claudio as a pain merchant. He would do whatever was necessary to get what he wanted, but he was not looking for an excuse for a bit of fun. To that extent at least the situation was under my control, but that was the best you could make of it, and it was not much.

The trouble was I felt such a bloody fool, to myself and, above all, to Lisa Gaston, and whatever I did was not likely to change that. If I turned up with a few finger-nails missing, it might alter her attitude, but it would not alter her judgement. It seemed that the best I could hope for was to sell Claudio a false line and be ahead of him again before he found it was false. But I was not at all sure I could manage it. For that matter, I was not at all sure I could make him believe even the truth. The monkey's head was familiar and accepted gospel to me by now, but yielded under duress and looked at in hot blood it did not sound very probable or very complete. I did not even know whether, if he believed he had what he wanted, he would leave me alive. Even if he did not deliberately kill me, as I was pledged to kill him, he would at least have to ensure himself a day or two's start, and that might leave me with a very narrow chance of survival. My mind threshed about in the darkness round my head, and returned always to the black conclusion that there was nothing for me to decide because it was not me, or at

110

any rate not my rational self, that was going to do the deciding.

I do not know how long this went on. If Claudio kept to his timing, it cannot in fact have been much more than a quarter of an hour, though I find that almost impossible to believe. It ended because suddenly, like the Ancient Mariner and equally unexpectedly, I heard two voices in the air. Two voices, and then footsteps, and then the door groaned again. A man's voice said, "God, it's dark inside. Come on, we haven't got long."

As in the poem, the other was a softer voice, as soft as honey-dew, but it did not say anything about anyone's doing penance. It made a short statement which the man greeted with an appreciative chuckle. It was a statement of physical fact so direct and appalling that even at my time of life I cannot bring myself to put it down on paper. I can only say that if I had not in any case had nowhere to look, I should not have known where to. I suppose it was the outraged convention in me that made me say the perfectly conventional thing. I cleared my throat and said, "Er—excuse me."

The girl made an indeterminate noise noticeably lacking in honey-dew, whatever that is, and the man said, "Christ."

I had to put my message across very quickly and succinctly. My sickening, overwhelming fear was that they might simply turn and bolt. I said, "Help me. Please help me. I'm tied up. You must untie me."

There was a moment's silence while my life, perhaps in cold truth, hung in the balance, and then the man made up his mind. He might speak with the terrible intonation of the north-western home counties, but he had after all the right stuff in him. He said, "Here, wait a minute. I've got a torch." There was another moment's silence, in which the light presumably found me, though I could still see nothing through

111

the total opacity of the bag. Then he said, "Christ," again, but this time his voice was close in front of me. He said, "What—?" but I cut him very short indeed.

"There's no time to ask questions," I said. "The man who tied me up will be back soon, and he's dangerous. Be a good chap and untie the ropes and get this damned bag off me, and let's all get to hell out of here."

He made up his mind very quickly now. "Okay, okay," he said. "You hold the light, and I'll have a go." This was presumably addressed to the girl, but it worried me a little.

I said, "Don't wave the light about more than you need. I haven't seen this place, but I expect a light shows outside, and we don't want him coming back at the double."

The man's hands were busy on the rope round me and the post, and his voice came from just outside the bag. "Doesn't, though," he said. "The windows are all boarded up. You can't see out at all."

The girl, almost equally close, but on the other side, giggled and said, "Or in. There's even a bolt on the door." She made it sound all very well appointed. If she had said there was h. and c. in every b., I should hardly have been surprised, except for the smell. I offered no comment. I found her conversation a bit beyond me altogether.

The man said, "Christ, these knots are hard. Who tied you up, King-Kong?"

"I told you he was dangerous," I said. "Do your best, and for God's sake be quick."

"I'm doing my best." He said it almost between his teeth. "Really need a knife. Save a lot of time."

"I may have one," I said, but I had not really much hope. "In a sheath behind my right hip."

His hand went up under the bottom of the bag and

groped. "Sheath all right," he said. "No knife. King-Kong must have had it."

I said, "Sorry," because I felt an apology was called for, over this and much else.

The girl said suddenly, "I've got a knife."

The man and I spoke together and both said the same thing. We both said, "*You* have?" It was a sort of simultaneous explosion of masculine incredulity. The man added, "What do you want a knife for, then?"

She said, "To cut things with. It's small but quite sharp. It's in my bag." She was tantalising him, but I had no patience for this.

"Then get it out," I said. "Get it out quick and give it to him. You really are in danger here. Not only me, you. Give it to him, please." I almost added, "there's a good girl," but she plainly had no wish to be taken for anything of the sort, and I did not want to affront her.

Even so, she snorted. "What have I done to King-Kong, then?" she said. But she must have handed over the knife, because the man stopped wrestling with the knots. I did not try explaining to her Claudio's probable views on what they were doing.

"Cor," the man said, "proper ladies' model." There was a new, gentle vibration on the rope. "Quite right, though," he said. "It's sharp, all right. What do you want—?" but this time I almost shouted at him.

"Never mind," I said. "You can have all that out afterwards. Get on with the cutting."

"Am," he said, "quick as I can. But I don't want to break the knife. You haven't seen it." Then something gave, and he jerked at the remaining fibres, and I was suddenly free of that damned post.

I think I staggered a bit. I had been standing, of course,

113

since Claudio left me, but it was some time since I had had
the free use of my legs, and I still had the bag over my head.
He gripped my arm through the stuff of the bag as Claudio
had done. It was almost a child's grip by comparison, but
much more friendly. "Steady on," he said. "Let's get this lot
off. Ah, thinner this time." I could have told him that
Claudio, or King-Kong, would have needed lighter stuff for
his noose-work in the car, but it was probably nylon, and certainly no easier to cut. As it was, I left him to it. I suppose in
my impatience I strained outwards on the rope, because he
said, "Easy, easy. If you tighten it like that, it's as hard as a
board, and I'm still scared of the knife going." I bit on my
impatience and let my arms go slack, and a few seconds later
he was helping me pull the bag over my head.

The only light I saw was that of the torch. It was pitch-
dark otherwise. The girl kept the light shining on my face, as
people often do without realising how devastatingly one-
sided the effect can be. Still, it was natural enough that they
should want to examine the contents of the surprise package
they had just unwrapped. Even if it no longer mattered, I
remember that I wanted to assure them of my respectability,
and even put up a hand instinctively to smooth down my
hair, which was tousled from the bag. Then I put the hand
over my eyes to shield them from the glare, and the man un-
derstood and said, "Here, don't blind the poor bugger now
he's got the use of his eyes back." He took the torch from
her and shone it upwards into the roof, and then we all
looked at each other in a dim whitish glow of indirect lighting. I confess it was the girl I looked at first, I think out of
pure human curiosity. She cannot have been more than sev-
enteen, and could have been even younger. She had a mop
of fair hair that shone in the torchlight, and what looked like
fresh colouring and pale eyes that could have been blue. Her

full, soft mouth was as unformed as a child's and as innocent as a cherub's. Fair Chloe, I thought, but Rochester's Chloe, fresh from the pig-sty. She was still smiling at the novelty of it all. By daylight she was probably an English rose, a bit forced in the bud, maybe, but very pluckable. The man was older and more ordinary. I think he was dark and pale-faced, but I did not waste much time on him.

I said, "Look, I haven't got time to thank you. I don't know who you are, and you don't know who I am, and let's just forget about it. But get right away from here quick, and don't come back again tonight, wherever you've come from. And if you see a big, red-faced man anywhere around, give him a wide berth. Now let's all get out, but put that light out before you open the door."

The man looked at me very hard for a moment, I think just to make sure I was in earnest. Then he said, "Right. Come on, girl." He shepherded her to the door and I went after them, leaving the bag and the cut ropes where they were. The door must have groaned when he opened it, but I did not notice it. There was still a gleam of daylight in the sky, but it was dark enough on the ground. We were on a small hill with the ground falling away all round us. I could see the beginning of the track going down to the lane on one side, and on the other a cluster of lights at the foot of the hill.

I pointed to them. "What's that?" I said, and the man said "Stonham."

The name meant nothing to me, but I nodded. "Village?" I said, and he said "Sort of," as if he did not think much of it.

"One pub or two?" I said, and he said, "Just the one."

"Is that where you'll be going?"

"Got to," he said. "The car's there."

115

"Can you go straight to it?"

"Can and will," he said. "That's the way we came."

"All right. Off you go, then. I'll go the other way. And remember what I said about the big man."

"I will," he said, and I thought he would, too. He seemed a sensible chap. I was sorry to have spoiled their evening, but it was dark now, and they had a car. I felt sure they would manage something. I nodded, and turned, and started off down the track.

I went very cautiously indeed, listening ahead all the time. I thought Claudio would come back by the way he had gone, because he probably had not explored the other approaches, and the distances were small anyway. The odds were all to nothing that he would have taken the car to the village and parked it outside the pub. He had probably gone in and had a pint—I was also willing to bet that he was a beer-drinker for choice—and then when he was ready, or when he reckoned I was, he would leave the car where it was and come back to the cottage on foot. Would have left, rather. If he was keeping to his timing, he must be nearly here by now. The track had thin scrubby hedges on each side, and I went down it almost foot by foot, looking all the time for cover when I needed it, and keeping my ears cocked ahead.

I was almost at the bottom when I heard his feet on the tarmac of the lane. He was coming steadily, but not hurrying, though he would walk with a long stride. I slid myself through a gap in the hedge and lay down flat on the far side. Even now I never saw him at all. I heard him go past me up the track. I gave him as much distance as I dared, and then went down the rest of the track onto the tarmac. Once there, I ran like hell. He would be in the cottage any time now, and would find enough to occupy him for a minute or two. He presumably had a light, to see what he had to do.

KILL CLAUDIO

Very likely he had matches or a lighter, and a cigarette or two, even if he did not smoke them himself.

As I thought it would, the lane curved round the foot of the hill and made for the village. I was badly blown by the time I got there, but I ran on, not minding if anyone saw me or what they would think if they did. I saw the pub sign and made for it in a final burst. The Crown, it was. There were half-a-dozen cars parked at the side, mine among them. Claudio must have had his own key, or one that would serve. He was well up to that. Mine was still in my trouser pocket. He had seen no reason to take it, and had not. I did not know where I was, but I could ask my way to the motorway presently. For the moment the thing was to put a couple of miles between me and Stonham.

I thought poor old Claudio, ill-meaning, but curiously innocent, as ever. I did not know how he had found the cottage, but anyone but a man innocent of country ways would have known that it was bound to be used for fornication once or twice an evening, especially on a Sunday. It was probably known to the youth for miles around. I did not know how he would get back to London, but if worse came to worst, perhaps the Crown would have a bed for him. I still wanted to know what the girl used her knife for, and wished I had not been so fierce with the man when he had tried to ask her. But maybe I was an innocent too.

117

CHAPTER 11.

Lisa Gaston came to London a fortnight later, this time by arrangement, though the suggestion came from her. I had given her a slightly edited version of my brush with Claudio and of my Sunday-evening adventures at Wimbledon and elsewhere. I had edited them, not at the expense of any essential detail, or even in mitigation of my own unimpressive performance on both occasions, but more to play down the elements of pure farce which I was very conscious of in both. I did not want her to think that I to any degree lacked seriousness in what was for her an immensely serious business. I knew it was serious myself. I knew that it might at some point involve my driving my new knife into Claudio's back. (I had replaced the one he had taken off me, and not this time with a sham war souvenir). But I was conscious of a change of attitude in myself, which I could not disguise from myself, but could not confess to Lisa. To put it at its simplest, perhaps even to over-simplify it, I was no longer, so far as Claudio was concerned, on the offensive. I still needed the money, if money there was under the monkey's head, but if I could have got it without killing Claudio, I would gladly have done so. I even think that if I had been faced with a straight choice between killing him and letting him have what he had so long wanted, and no intermediate course offered itself, I should, left to myself, have let him have it. I knew that I should not be left to myself, because there was

118

Lisa Gaston, and I did not want to be left without her, but the personal preference remained. Even in the matter of simple retribution I felt I had the right to differ from her. She wanted Claudio killed be ause he had killed Peter. For myself, I was conscious of the fact that his killing of Peter had been a not uncharacteristic blunder. It had been me he had intended to kill, and I felt it was up to me to decide whether or not he should be killed in retaliation for my intended murder. Peter was dead now, and killing Claudio could not bring him back. I was very much alive, and killing Claudio could not make me any more so. And there was something in the man, dangerous and probably unbalanced as he was, that I did not care about killing.

Lisa came to London by train on Saturday, and got a room at a hotel near the terminus. She was to come to me a bit before noon on Sunday, by which time I could have had a few hours' sleep, which was all I needed with the prospect of a full night's sleep ahead. I did not propose, this time, to receive her in pyjamas and dressing-gown, still less with a gun in my hand and an unmade bed in the background. I got up at eleven, tidied myself and the room, put out the coffee things and sat down to wait for the agreed pattern of knocks on the door. This business of knocking to an agreed formula is one of the few fictional commonplaces that is genuinely useful in practice. Short of some wild coincidence, like the combination of drunken Doones which would have cost Lorna her virginity but for the timely and characteristically violent arrival of John Ridd, it is fool-proof, can be rejigged for each occasion and is capable of infinite variations. If both parties know morse, it can be based on an easily remembered combination of letters, and you can then have a standing formula, such as the first two letters of the day of the week, which will hold good even if the visit is unexpected. Lisa, to my gratification but not particularly to my surprise, apparently did know Morse, and had said she would knock the letter L. The L-shaped knock came in fact a couple of minutes before noon, and I opened the door with a smile of welcome which was frozen immediately by the look on her face as she came in.

She came straight in, waited until I had shut and locked the door and then said, "I think I've just met Claudio."

I asked the essential question. The where and the how could wait. I said, "Did he recognise you?"

She thought for a moment, but when it came her answer was quite decisive. "No," she said. "Not unless he's a pretty skilled dissimulator, and Peter said he's not."

I said, "Thank God for that. How did it happen?"

"I came round the back of the block. I didn't want to come direct from the tube-station in case there was anyone watching. I turned up the side-street to the west of the block to get to the front. There weren't many people about. I was half-way up it when I saw this man coming toward me. He must have turned into the street from the front of the block a little after I'd turned in from the back. The more I saw of him, the less I liked it, but there was nothing I could do, just keep on walking. We met and passed. I slowed my pace, so that he could reach his corner before I reached mine. I gave him as much time as I dared, and then risked a quick look back. He hadn't stopped, and didn't turn round himself, or not when I was looking at him. He went on and turned the corner. Then I knew at least that he couldn't see me come here, so I got around to the front and came in as quickly as I could."

I nodded. "Would he recognise you again?" I said.

She thought about this. She even smiled slightly. "He might," she said. "He's one for the ladies, is Claudio. He

120

made good view of me, you know? I can't say that sure me-
thought his eyes had lost his tongue, because we weren't on
speaking terms. But he didn't miss much. Well, he may look
at half the women he meets like that. But if he saw me with
you, say, or somewhere where he knew you were around, the
penny might just drop. At least it's a thing we should bear in
mind."

"All right," I said. "Sit down and tell me about him. I
know he's big and red-faced. I suspect he's a natty dresser,
which rather goes with what you say about him. Tell me
about his face, the way he looks."

She considered this too, frowning slightly, I thought not so
much from distaste as because something puzzled her. Finally she smiled again, slightly but unmistakably. "The
funny thing is," she said, "I rather liked the look of him. I
even wondered after I had passed him whether it really had
been Claudio, but on your account of him it must have been,
especially being where he was. And don't think I was melted
by his apparent admiration. There was no sex-attraction in it
at all. It was—I don't know—a sort of slightly ridiculous
charm, a bit like a large young animal, rather taking even if
you know it's dangerous. The danger is there, all right. It
shows in the eyes, I think."

I felt a curious sense of relief, as if the heresy, or even
treachery, I had been conscious of was after all venial. All I
said was, "What sort of eyes?"

"Big and blue and rather staring, as if they were seeing
more than was really there. I don't think he's very closely in
touch with reality, do you know? His picture of himself is
what counts. That goes with his clothes, too, and his too obvious gallantry. As I said, he sees himself as a ladies' man,
but in fact he's almost completely unattractive. One couldn't

121

take him seriously, not in that way, I mean. In other ways, yes."

I ventured the word which had been in my mind earlier. "Immature?" I said. "Big and powerful, but immature?" and she nodded at once.

"That's probably it," she said. "He even looks young in a sort of way, which he can't really be. I mean, he was a grown man twenty years back."

I let my cat a little further out of the bag, as it were, to meet hers. "It's in the voice, too." I said. "You've seen him and I've heard him. He's got rather a light, high voice for a man of his size. He talks like a young Wiltshire policeman." I almost added, "And you still want him killed?" but I knew I must not say that yet. Instead I said, "What about the rest of his face?"

"Oh—big, of course. Pink and fleshy. And he sports a big fair moustache. Not handle-bars, but certainly not tooth-brush. What you might call full Edwardian."

I had the physical picture now, almost as complete and vivid as if I had seen him myself, and still I could not put a name to him. I remembered him now as a person, or thought I did—I mean, remembered him from twenty years back. I remembered the impression he had made on us, myself and other members of the Establishment, the almost involuntary liking you had for him, always conditioned by the feeling that he was not to be taken too seriously or trusted too far. But although I now knew pretty well what he looked like, and he probably had not changed much, I still could not put a face to the man I thought I remembered, or find a face among my remembered faces that looked like Claudio, or a name among my remembered names that went with a face like that. I sat with my eyes on the floor, frowning probably in the concentrated effort to remember, and at last lifted my eyes and looked at Lisa and shook my head. "I still can't place him," I said. "It's no good. And yet I remember there was a man like that, not his appearance, I mean, the sort of man he was. I can remember this feeling of half liking him. It was the only thing I could remember after reading Peter's letter, and it's been getting clearer all the time, and now you say the same. It's odd, isn't it?"

She sat there staring at me in that disconcerting, deadpan way she had, as if she was very much aware of you, but was thinking entirely of what you had said and not at all of you as a person. It seemed a disturbingly unfeminine trick in so intensely feminine a person, so that I always felt an urge somehow to call attention to myself, but did not know how to when she was already looking at me. All I could do was wait, but I waited a little unhappily. Finally she said, "Odd, yes. But he's still dangerous, you know."

I smiled at her. I was determined to re-establish the contact which she had momentarily but effectively suspended. I said, "I'm not likely to forget that. Not after what happened the Sunday before last. Whatever sort of a person he is, he can still frighten me. And at the moment, he's making the running."

She nodded and then sat forward suddenly in her chair, so suddenly and decisively that I thought for a moment she was going to get up, but she did not. She said, "I think that's what we've got to stop. That's really why I came." She looked at me for a moment. Then she said, "When can you go?"

"Any time now," I said, "given a fortnight's notice."

She said, "Well, give it, then. This has been going on long enough." She thought for a moment. "How will you go?" she said. "Boat or plane?"

I was watching her very carefully, not quite sure what she

123

had in mind and, as usual, desperately anxious not to make any false assumptions. But her face told me nothing, and I had to know. "I think that depends," I said.

"On what?"

"On whether you have it in mind to come too."

Her eyebrows went up in real surprise. "Of course I'm coming," she said. Then she smiled at me, a perfectly friendly, open smile. "Along with you," she said, "but not in your company."

I smiled back at her with equal friendliness. "Good," I said. "Then boat, and probably along with Claudio, though I trust not in his company. The planes are pretty small. He couldn't travel on the same plane, and then I should have to wait till he showed up on the island. I couldn't even be certain he was there, and I'd have to know. If we all go by boat, he could see me safely aboard, and you could see him safely aboard, and then we should know where we all were. I mean you and I should. I'm assuming he wouldn't know where you were, or even who you were. You can manage that?"

"Oh, surely," she said. "I shan't wear dark glasses or a blond wig, but I shan't be looking at all as I am now."

I said, "You look very nice now." It was true, too, and I did not see why I should not say it, even if it was not strictly relevant to the matter in hand. She was not, as I have said, a beauty, or even in any obvious way pretty, but she could look very elegant, and looked elegant now. Dressed for town, I thought, or had reluctantly to suppose it was for town. I was not surprised Claudio had looked her over, especially in the part of town I lived in. She was looking at me, pleased, I was prepared to swear she was pleased, but a little doubtfully. I said, "Admiration where admiration's due. I'm not just being a ladies' man like Claudio."

She said perfectly seriously, "You're not in the least like

124

Claudio. So far as that goes, the opposite. You're very male, but keep it very much to yourself." She looked away from me, and then gave me a quick glance and away again. "I sometimes wonder about you," she said.

I assumed the question which I had to assume, or at any rate assumed, she was asking. "I manage," I said. "Or have up to now. But no personal commitments at all."

She looked at me again and shook her head slightly. "I'm not sure I like the sound of that," she said. "But it's no business of mine."

I thought of little Tamara, whom I had not seen all these months, and knew that it was in fact very much Lisa's business, but I could not say so, perhaps not ever, certainly not yet. I said, "I'm sorry, I'm afraid we've wandered from the point, and it was my fault."

She smiled at me. "Don't apologise," she said. "I enjoyed the detour. And thank you for the compliment. The truth is, I don't often dress up these days, and it's nice to know I still can without going wrong. Peter never missed a trick on clothes. Women's clothes, I mean. He didn't dress up much himself. I'd miss his critical eye even if I had anything or anyone to dress up for."

I smiled back at her. I said, "You've got Claudio, the ladies' man. You might even find a use for that, so long as he didn't know who you were. And for what it's worth, you've got me. Not, I hope, a ladies' man, but a woman's man, as you rightly say, if the woman wants me. Not otherwise."

She had half-turned in her chair and was staring out of the window, though from where we were there was nothing to see but sky. She spoke suddenly in a different voice, one of her voices I had heard before, almost as if she was talking to herself. She said, "I heard a radio programme the other day. We—I haven't got television. Peter wouldn't have it. But I

125

listen to radio quite a lot now. One of those heart-throb programmes, bare your bosom and tell the truth, you know. There were four women, all widows, and the usual oily-voiced man asking them about their experience of widowhood. I suppose that's why I listened. It wasn't the sort of thing I usually listen to. He asked them what they missed the most, and they all produced suitably touching answers, and all of them dishonest as hell. Not one of them, not one of the silly bitches, said she missed her husband in bed. Perhaps it's so obvious it doesn't need saying. The trouble is, I'm still in love with Peter, and he's dead."

For a moment or two we neither of us said anything. I think I was holding my breath. Then I said, "So you should be. I knew Peter, and he was worth loving. Perhaps some time, when you've got over the worst of your unhappiness, we might talk about it again. But not till then. Or not so far as I'm concerned." I thought for a moment. "And if it's any comfort to you," I said, "that surprises me as much as it may you."

She turned then and looked full at me, her dark eyes very wide. She said, "Thank you, Ben. I haven't been paid a compliment like that, not for a very long time. I shan't forget it."

I smiled at her and spoke with a lightness I did not at all feel. I said, "Well, that's good. So long as you understand. So long as we both understand. Now let's get back to Claudio, the ladies' man, but still dangerous."

We made our plans then, as far as we could make them at that stage. I was to get my dates fixed and find out the name of a hotel on the island, preferably the biggest, but in any case as big as possible. When I had let her know, we were to write independently and each book a room for a week from the agreed date. We were to book in our real names, anything else being complicated and unnecessary. Claudio

126

would almost certainly see me to my hotel, in any case. Once the bookings were confirmed, we should make our own independent travel arrangements, converging on the night boat to the island. On the boat we should get cabins, single if possible, and make no attempt to communicate except in emergency, one agreed emergency being if Claudio did not seem to be on board. Once on shore, I was to take a taxi to the hotel, and Lisa was to have a hired self-drive car waiting for her and follow Claudio, first probably to our hotel and then if possible to wherever he chose to hole up himself. She was then to come to our hotel and check in, and we could then get in touch by internal telephone. I myself would hire a self-drive car as soon as I had breakfasted and settled in. The rest could wait.

It was well into the afternoon when we finished, and we ate the scratch lunch I had got in for the occasion. It was the best my tiny refrigerator could manage, but did at least include a bottle of white Hermitage, which was the most expensive bottle I had bought for a long time, but fully justified the price I had paid for it. It was a friendly occasion altogether. It was as if we both felt a sense of a tension resolved and a burden of doubt lifted. What this was I do not think either of us could have said, but it had very little to do with our plans for Claudio and the island. We drank our coffee, and then Lisa said, exactly as she had the first time, 'I must be going now. There's a train I can catch."

I did not try to keep her. I do not think I even wanted to. Between us, for the moment, there was nothing more to be said. I wanted above all to be alone and think things over. When she was ready to go, she said, "Better give me the gun. You won't want it on the journey, and if there is a check, I can manage it better than you can. But unloaded, please." I did not ask her how she would manage. I found I

127

trusted her completely in things like that, and my own recent record did not inspire much confidence in the matter of keeping my weaponry out of enemy hands. She smiled when I dug the Colt and its precious ammunition from under the floor-board, but did not say anything. I emptied the magazine and worked the slide to eject the remaining round from the breech. She put the lot into her handbag. It was a capacious leather bag with a sling strap, handsome enough in itself, but not really going with her towny elegance. I thought she had come prepared to collect the gun, and had now collected it.

At the door she said, "Will he be watching, do you think?"

"Not very likely," I said. "It's too late for me to go out walking now, and I didn't go last Sunday. In any case, he won't know where you've come from. But I'll check to the top of the stairs."

I opened the door and tiptoed to the end of the empty landing. Mrs. Iacovou's door was shut, and there was the familiar noise of a family reunion going on inside. I came back and said, "All clear." It was exactly as it had been the first time, only just as she went out, she put out a hand and touched mine. I watched her to the head of the stairs and then went in and locked the door behind me.

CHAPTER 12.

The hotel window, as advertised, commanded extensive sea
views, which at the moment were the last thing I wanted it
to. I would have settled for an endless rolling plain, always
so long as it did not actually roll. The main front of the
building faced east, with only the width of the street between it and the sea-wall. Beyond the wall the grey sea
heaved sullenly in the lee of the land and further out broke
intermittently in foam where the north-west wind swooped
down on it again from over the height of the island. To the
right harbour and castle huddled under the driving rain, and
in front two smaller islands, one low-lying and fairly near
and the other steep-to and much further away, took the sea
in an unending flurry of white on their weather shores. I had
a good and solid hotel breakfast inside me, and no longer felt
actually sick, but there was a dull ache in my temples, and
the awful depression of sea-sickness still hung over me like a
cloud. If Claudio had been in the hotel, I would willingly
have phoned him and told him all I knew and wished him
luck and taken the next available plane back to the mainland. But I did not know where Claudio was. I had to assume that he had been on the boat, or I should have heard
from Lisa before now, provided, of course, she had been on
the boat herself. I did not know even that for certain. I had
not seen her on the boat, and she had not appeared in the
hotel dining-room while I had my breakfast. I felt certain of

nothing but my own slowly dying misery. I knew that it was dying, and that I should feel less abject presently, but for the moment abject was what I still felt.

I came away from the window and sat down on the bed and looked at the telephone on the bedside table. I thought it was time I tried a call to Lisa's room, but I did not know what state she was in herself, even supposing she was there at all. I could not reconcile my picture of her with the total abandon of sea-sickness, but I knew sea-sickness was no respecter of persons. The fatuous, dangerous Claudio was not subject to it, as I remembered from my last visit to the island twenty years before, but I could not be sure of Lisa. She had not appeared at breakfast, but that might only have meant that she was competently carrying out the agreed manoeuvres while I was struggling to rehabilitate myself in the stable comfort of the hotel. I hesitated for a moment, and then, as I reached out for the telephone, the bell rang suddenly under my outstretched hand.

I picked up the receiver and gave my room number, and Lisa's voice said, "Mr. Selby?"

"Yes," I said, "yes. How are you, Lisa?"

"Me?" She sounded slightly puzzled. "I'm fine. And you?"

"Better now. I was ghastly seasick."

She said, "Oh, no. I'm so sorry." There was not even a touch of the good sailor's jocularity on the subject. She was all real concern. "Why didn't you take something?"

"Do you know, I simply didn't think of it. I was a fool, of course. But I haven't been sea-borne for years, and flying does nothing to me. It was dead calm when I left London. It simply never occurred to me to worry until the damned ship started to pitch, and by then it was too late. But forget it. I'm almost over it."

She said again, "I'm sorry. I know it's hellish. I'm just lucky."

I said, "So's Claudio."

"You haven't seen him?" Her voice was very sharp and immediate.

"Not this time, no. But twenty years ago he was immune, so I suppose he still is. I take it he is with us?"

"Yes, yes. I picked him up at the ferry terminal, waiting for your train to come in. I must say, it makes him very easy to keep track of, his being the size he is. You just look for a head standing clear of all the other heads and wearing its hat a bit on one side, and that's Claudio. Once he'd seen you aboard, he went and telephoned, and then went aboard himself. I brought up the rear."

I said, "I wonder who the hell he telephoned, and what about? He hasn't got a side-kick, has he? I've always assumed not."

"No," she said, "I think I know what it was. I'll tell you. This morning, when we berthed, I wanted to be ashore ahead of you, and made for the gangway entry-port as soon as I'd found out where it was. I was well up in the queue, in fact, but he was ahead of me, almost flattening his nose on the doors. He never looked round, but if he had, he wouldn't have recognised me. I went down the gang-way with half-a-dozen people between me and him. After that it was almost funny, really, though it mightn't have been. There were only two pre-hired cars waiting, both exactly alike, one for him and one for me. I reckon that's what he phoned about, once he knew you were on board. He wanted to make sure of being able to follow you without any of the driver-follow-that-cab stuff, which I suppose might sound a bit unusual in a place like this. Anyway, there we were, and by the grace of God he tackled his own driver first. I mean, my man could so easily have said, 'No, I'm for a Mrs. Mowbray,' and that really must have made him think. As it was, he got involved in the formalities without so much as looking at me. I'd got through all mine by post, paid my deposit and all that. I merely showed the man my driving licence, and I was away. I drove just clear of the berth and pulled in and waited. I reckon he took over his car, and left it there, and went back to see you off the boat. When you made for the taxis, he must have run back to it and followed you. Anyway, presently along you both came, you in your taxi and Claudio driving himself in his hire car two cars behind you, and I just pulled out and fell in behind, with a car between me and him. It was quite a procession. When your taxi pulled up to the hotel, he didn't stop at all, just slowed down long enough to make sure of you, and then was off like a rocket along the sea-front with me after him. It was a bit of a chase, and the island roads are pretty lethal. I tell you one thing. He's been here before, I mean since your original landing. He knows the ground all right. I imagine he's got the actual headland identified, because I think that's where he's staying, or as near as he can. It's about half-way along the north-west coast. A rather dubious little hotel, but no doubt commanding good views. If he's near enough, he's only got to sit in his window with a pair of field-glasses, and he's got the place covered. Of course, he had to know where you were staying and all that, but there's no reason why he should come into town after you. You can't do any harm here. He can just wait for you to come to him."

I thought about this for a moment. Then I said, "No, Lisa, he's not sitting quite as pretty as that. He can't be sure which headland the thing's on, or even that it's on a headland at all. The first time we saw Peter after the wreck, he was on the beach, and by then he'd already hidden it. You and I know it's on the headland we actually struck on, because we've got Peter's story, but Claudio can't, unless Peter talked a lot more clearly in the ambulance than seems likely. All I've got to do is find the bay, take the headland on its western side and look for the monkey's head. But for all Claudio knows, the thing can be anywhere fairly close to the bay, on either headland or even inland above the beach. He can't know where Peter got ashore. He can only watch my movements, and he's got quite an area to watch."

"Yes," she said, "you're probably right. That's good. So—what do you propose?"

"First, do what we agreed, go out and hire a car for myself. As different from yours as possible, I think. Then we could always switch cars if the occasion arose, and it might fox him for a bit."

"You can try, but I don't think you'll find it easy. As far as I can make out, they're all Minors, and they've all got an H before the number. The actual numbers are different, obviously, and I imagine they must come in different colours. Mine's a plain grey. It's parked outside the hotel. If you can get something noticeably different, a black or a red, say, and let him identify it as yours, you might if need be leave it parked outside the hotel or somewhere equally obvious, and then pick up mine from somewhere else. I'd better not use yours if it can be avoided, because he'd only have to see me in it to know I was working with you, and we want to avoid that at all costs."

"I agree about that, of course," I said. "In any case, I don't want you taking my place in the firing line. Not that there's going to be any firing, at any rate not yet. If I actually got there first, anything could happen, with Claudio's mind in the state it is. But that's for the future. All right. I'll go out and get my obviously different hire car. Then I'm go-

133

ing to take a drive along the north-west coast and try to identify my headland. That shouldn't be too difficult, unless
things have changed a lot in twenty years. They will have a
bit, of course. But there's a tower inland from the beach that
lines up with the house our rescuers lived in, and I expect
the tower's still there, at least. I won't go on the headland, of
course. I won't even stop there if I can help it. If you're
right, Claudio will pick up my car from his hotel, or wherever he's watching from, and I'll give him a good chance to
see me in or near it, so that he'll identify it as mine. That will
be enough for today, I think. I think the next thing will be to
get to the headland itself in the darkness, preferably in the
very early morning. I could leave my car well away inland
and go on foot, and wait for daylight to do a bit of detailed
exploration. After all, it was at first light that Peter saw the
monkey's head, and close to this time of the year. But I've
got to get to the end of the headland without Claudio's
knowing I'm there, and I've got to know the ground first.
Anyhow, for today a pleasant drive by that blasted wild sea,
and let the dog see the rabbit. Do you agree? If so, there'll
be nothing for you to do today except keep your head down.
You have a quiet day. You've earned it even if you don't
need it. I'll report as soon as I'm back, and then we can set-
tle the next move in more detail. All right?"

"Yes," she said, "yes, I suppose so. All right, you go ahead,
and I'll hear from you later. But be careful, won't you?"

"I'll be careful, all right. But he isn't going to kill me yet,
not until I've led him to what he wants, and I'm not giving
him another chance to nobble me, I can promise you that.
Oh, by the way, what's it called, this hotel he's in?"

"It's called the Grande Hougue, but that must be a place-
name. The hotel's small enough. It's right on the coast-road,

facing the sea. You can't miss it if you follow the road. Good luck, then, Ben."

I said, "Talk to you later, Lisa. Perhaps even see you across the room at dinner. It'll be better than nothing." I put the receiver down before she needed to think what to say.

I walked past Lisa's car on the way out and memorised the number. The island numbers had no letters to them, so the H must be special to hire-cars. The colour was a stand-ard Morris grey. It was not the only grey thing about, not by a long chalk. The whole world seemed grey, sky and sea and wet tarmac and the massive granite of the sea-wall. The rain had stopped, but even here among the houses and under the lee of the island the wind seemed stronger than ever. I remembered when I was a child hearing talk of equinoctial gales, and thought perhaps this was what we were working up for, if such things really exist. It was no doubt not a gale yet in any strict sense, but to a committed landsman like me there seemed plenty of wind about, and I knew there would be more on the other side of the island. How conditions com-pared with those at the time of our wreck twenty years before I could not say, but I felt grateful to Peter for leaving a purely land operation on my hands.

I found my way to the address Lisa had given me and said I wanted to hire a car for a week. The man said certainly, sir, no problem. It was well past the holiday season, of course, and he was probably glad of a customer. The garage seemed full of Minors with H numbers, and all the ones I could see were grey. It was probably the firm's uniform, and I had a feeling I should have done better to try somewhere else, only that would have wasted time. He said, "Just for yourself, sir? A Minor will be all right?"

I had not got a rational explanation to offer, but I thought probably with him that would not matter. I said, "A Minor will be fine, only I've got a thing against grey cars. Have you got one of a different colour?" I looked suitably deprecating and slightly foolish, as if I knew I was being unreasonable.

He looked at me a bit sharply, all the same. He said, "Had trouble with a grey car, then, sir?" He was wondering about my driving record, as he was fully entitled to.

"Not a car," I said. "I've never had a grey one. Just grey in general. I never back grey horses. Some people back them all the time." I made a rather silly joke of it, and he relaxed a little.

He said, "I'm afraid all our Minors are grey. It's our colour." Then he brightened up, and I felt certain I knew the way his mind was working. The customer is always right, but there's no reason why he should not pay for the privilege. "I tell you what," he said. "We've got a blue Triumph. It's not one of our regular hire-cars, but I could let you have it for a week. Only it'll cost you a bit more, I'm afraid."

I smiled at him, he was so pleasant in his simple commerciality. "I'll back my fancy," I said. "Roll out your Triumph. A week won't break me." At least I hoped it would not, and the more different from Lisa's car the better. It was worth paying for.

We completed the transaction amid pleasant badinage about what terrible weather it was for my first visit to the island, and about twenty minutes later I got into my blue Triumph and headed out of town. The number had no H on it. Whether he was taking a chance with the police I did not know, but if he was I expect he had made it worth his while. The only thing I wondered about was how to interest Claudio in what did not look like a hire car. I might have to be a bit obvious about it, but it ought to be possible. I had done my work on a large-scale map, and followed, up to a point, the main road running almost due west out of town.

Only up to a point, because if I followed it through to the north-west coast, I thought it would be likely to bring me out so near my probable objective that I should not know, when I reached the coast-road, which way I had to turn. I preferred to come out further west, so that I knew I had only to turn right and follow the coast-road, and I was bound to come to it sooner or later. Also, I had a mind, if I could, to get a comprehensive view of the stretch of coast with which I was concerned. For this I needed to get up to the highest part of the island, and I had found on the map a place from which, if I read the contours right, and there were no obstructions, I ought to be able to get the view I wanted. I therefore turned left and up-hill before I was well out of the town, leaving my original road to follow its long gradual descent to the coast.

I say before I was well out of the town, but I found myself, as I drove, increasingly doubtful whether I ever should be. The main shopping streets were confined to a tiny area round the harbour, but beyond this the built-up residential area seemed to go on indefinitely, so that I began to wonder whether there was any open country left on the island at all. It was all very green and pleasant and sleek and prosperous, but it was undeniably, by English standards, suburban. There were cars everywhere all the time. The traffic, as it had to be on these roads, was sedate and well disciplined, but it was almost continuous. I wondered what it must be like in the holiday season, when all the hire cars were out and about in the hands of exploring visitors. I found later that there were still tracts of green lanes and agricultural, or at least horticultural, land, but I never lost this first, bizarre impression of a well-oiled garden suburb, bounded by beautiful but dangerous coasts and set, incongruously but irretrievably, in the primeval wastes of the mere Atlantic. The island remains for me, on a grand scale, my vision of Wimbledon Common in reverse. I am not suggesting for a moment that this is a fair picture of the island or the way other people see it. But then no one with my fear of the sea would live on an island of that size anyway.

The rain had held off, but the higher I got, the more the wind hit me, and I was now driving directly into it. Whether I ever found my selected vantage point I am not sure, but at some point I came out over the brow of a hill, and there suddenly it all was, a mile or so from me and a few hundred feet below, the long, low lying, lethal north-west coast of the island, putting its head down, as it had since God knows when, into the perennial battering of wind and sea. Out to sea the rock reefs, black between grey sea and grey sky, threw up continual bursts of white spray as the sea broke over them, and further in, under the very edge of the inhabited land, the low green headlands reached out until they lost their last turf and fell away into splintered spines of rock, which themselves at last disappeared in the white smother of breaking water. Somewhere down there, twenty years ago, in the last dark hour of the night and in some such conditions as these the Establishment had lost a valuable consignment and a couple of presumably valuable lives. Somewhere down there, twenty years ago, I had had an experience which had changed my way of life, and which I had since tried hard not to think of. Now there was a man somewhere down there, a man who had shared my experience, and who had since apparently thought of very little else. I was on my way to him, not I hoped to meet him, but to engage his attention with a view to misleading him in his quest and ultimately, if need be, killing him. It was at this point, with the wind shaking the car and the sea playing hell

with the coastline below, that I remembered I had never got
Lisa's gun back.

CHAPTER 13.

I made a move to get out of the car, but the wind slammed the door shut again, and I thought better of it. I could see as much from inside the car as I could have from outside, and I could not, even so, see what I was in particular looking for. This was the tower I had once seen from the beach in the first light of day, behind and above the house we had had help from, but not all that far from it. As I now knew from the map, the coast of the island was full of towers and even forts, mostly dating from the years of danger from Napoleonic France, some refurbished in more recent wars, some altogether of more recent building. The one thing they had in common was that they had never been called on to fight off an invasion. The thing had always been settled elsewhere, and the expected invaders had either never come, or had come only to receive an already-acknowledged surrender. My tower, from what I remembered of it, could have been something in the nature of a Martello tower, possibly with later embellishments. It would stand high in relation to the flat land round it, but from up here it might hardly show at all. In any case, the whole coast inland from the road seemed to have been heavily and rather sadly built up in the past twenty years. I did not expect to find the house any longer standing alone above the bay, and the tower, though it was probably still there, might well be in the middle of a bunch of more or less deplorably bijou residences which would

140

mask it effectively from the higher ground. Even so, it would probably still get its head enough above them to be identifiable from a lower level, and all I could do was to go down there and hope to see it from the coast-road.

I started the car and drove on downhill towards that raging sea, no longer worrying about particular roads, but always, in case of doubt, taking a western fork rather than an eastern one. I knew I could get all the easting I wanted once I was on the coast-road itself. I finally came out onto it in the middle of a long curve where it negotiated the head of a bay. I turned right onto it, drove a short distance and then pulled the car onto the stretch of sandy turf which alone, at this point, separated the road from the sea-wall. I was fairly certain that this was not my bay, but it was time I got out and had a look at the whole terrain. I buttoned my mackintosh round me and clamped my hat firmly on my head. Then I stepped out into the wind and put my head over the wall.

The first thing that struck me in fact was less the force of the wind than the salt wetness of the air. It seemed to be about half-tide, though whether rising or falling I did not know. The sea was down clear of the stone beach, but coming in in long lines of breaking surf over the stretch of sand below it, and only a little below the stones there was a shambles of white seething water with the wind blowing in steadily over it. There was not much visible spray here, as there was on the rocks further out, but so much fragmented seawater in the wind that the air I breathed struck cold in my nostrils and smelt of nothing but salt. I found later, when I got back to the car, that the seaward side of it was already scurfed with a fine coating of salt, so that I had to use the windscreen washers to get a reasonable visibility before I drove on again. Meanwhile, as I had thought, this was clearly not my bay. Other things apart, it was much too wide and rounded. I thought the next one to the east might be mine, in which case the headland now on my right as I looked out to sea would be my ultimate objective. It was a long, low headland, turfed to about half its length, but capped all the way along by a great jagged spine of rock, so carved and splintered by wind and spray that it would not need much imagination to see the monkey's head capping any one of its upthrust spikes. There were not many houses where I was, and those there were set well back from the landward side of the road. Further east there seemed to be quite a jumble of buildings close to the road, and it was those, obviously, that I had to go on and look at. I could still see no sign of Claudio's hotel. The air was not really cold, but the whole place, in that grey light and ravaging wind, so bare and desolate that whatever the stakes I instinctively wanted no part of it. I turned my back on the sea and went and got into the car, but at once got out again to clear my near-side windows of salt. Finally, as I have said, I used the washers on the windscreen, and then started the engine and drove back onto the road, heading east.

The road ran through a small cutting in the base of the headland, so that the ground on my right was level with the tops of the craggy spine running seaward on my left, and someone who must have been a glutton for sea-views had built himself a house there. It was all picture windows and white pebble-dash under red tiles, fine when the sun was out and the sea a Mediterranean blue, but looking particularly gruesome in these conditions. And this was only the start. Other houses, in varying degrees of newness, but all relatively recent, closed in on the landward side of the road, as if someone, presumably with the permission of the authorities, had sold a sizeable strip of barren land in small lots to an eager builder, and no doubt done very well out of it. I was not

an islander, and it was no business of mine, but I thought all
the same that he must have thrown in most of his soul with
the land he sold, perhaps as an extra reflected in the price.
So closely packed were the houses that I drove another fifty
yards or so before I saw what I was looking for, a square
block of stone standing up among the variegated colours of
the pitched roofs under it like a dark rock in a momentarily
frozen Walt Disney sea. My tower was there all right, the
furthest seamark of my sail. I had arrived, and did not particularly welcome my arrival.

It was not, in fact, a square tower in the ordinary sense,
merely rectangular in elevation. It was probably a perfectly
ordinary round Martello tower, though for all I knew it had
since been tarted up and transformed into someone's holiday
cottage. But I never doubted its identity, and a moment
later I saw the house, too, a low stone house standing right
on the road and turning its back with understandable dignity on its raffish neighbours. I drove until the top of the
tower showed above the roof of the house, and then, with a
resolution I did not feel, pulled the car into the seaward side
of the road and stopped.

For the first time since I had started out, I wondered
where Claudio was. That he was not far off I had no doubt,
but I wondered precisely where. If he was at his hotel, he
was not particularly close to the scene of operations, because
there was nothing like a hotel on the road here. Further
ahead, it might be as much as a quarter of a mile, I could see
a two-storey building, probably of white-rendered stone
under a slate roof, which might well be a small hotel of the
older type with a small cluster of mostly single-storey houses
around it. There was only one small window high up in the
gable wall facing me, and if, as seemed probable, all the bedroom windows faced the sea, it was not, in fact, particularly

143

well fitted to survey what I at least knew to be important
ground. From a front window upstairs Claudio could no
doubt see the western headland if he looked that way, but he
would have to flatten his nose on the glass and squint sideways, or even open the window and lean out a little. The
first would be profoundly uncomfortable for a permanent
watch, and the second, in these conditions, all but impossible. I concluded that he had probably found himself a hide
somewhere nearer the bay, and with the land lying flat and
bare to the sea-wall and the beach lying flat and bare under
it, that would almost certainly have to be on one of the headlands, probably on the side facing the beach and not too far
out. Which headland he had chosen, I had no means of
knowing. The eastern headland was very different from the
western, flatter, greener and much less rocky, with what
looked like a small fort or blockhouse standing half-way
along it. If it was accessible, as no doubt to a man of
Claudio's size and agility it would be, the blockhouse would
be an admirable vantage-point, especially in these conditions. It was, of course, on the other side of the bay from the
actual objective, but he was not to know that, and in any
case the distances involved were small. Even if the tide was
well up, he could be off his headland and onto the other in a
matter of minutes if there was anything there that called for
closer investigation. I therefore settled for a working hypoth-
esis that he was in or near the blockhouse, no doubt with
field-glasses at the ready.

Meanwhile, I had two positive purposes and one negative
one. I wanted to have a good look at the western headland
without actually going out on it. I wanted Claudio to see me
and identify my car. And I did not want him to catch me,
particularly without my gun, in any place where he could
have another try at nobbling me without doing it in what

144

was, after all, an open and fairly populous place, with cars passing at regular intervals along the road. By way of killing the first two birds with one stone, I got out of the car and walked over to the sea-wall. Then, as it was only waist-high on the landward side, though much higher above the beach, I climbed up on top of it and stood there, leaning forward against the wind with my clothes flapping round me, and made a general and leisurely survey of the bay. It was only ostensibly a general survey, obviously. It was the western headland I was interested in, but I reckoned that even with the most powerful glasses Claudio could not possibly see, if he was watching me, which way my eyes were mainly directed.

The headland was a formidable piece of ground by any standards. Seawards, it ran out in a long line of jagged rocks, which got gradually lower and further separated from each other until they disappeared in the breaking sea. It would have been out at the end of this savage line, or near it, that the yacht had struck. This was all very much as Peter had described it, though how he had ever made his way to land along the reef, even at the cost of a badly knocked head, defied the imagination. I thought the wind had probably been a lot more westerly than it now was, and the tide certainly lower. That would give some shelter from the worst of the sea on the side nearer the bay, but even so he had been miraculously lucky to make it. Even when the rocks merged in the land, they did not lose their menace, and at one place, about half-way down the bay, the near side of the headland was nothing but a sheer wall of rock twenty or thirty feet high, which at high tide must fall straight into deep water, and even now overhung a welter of foam where the ends of the breakers pounded periodically over the scatter of small rocks at its foot. I thought that whatever I had to do when I

found my way out on to the headland, that was one place I
would keep clear of. Inland crags I could cope with if I had
to, but crags hanging over deep and turbulant water were
not for me. The top of the headland, once decisively clear of
the sea, seemed to consist of stretches of turf set at all angles
and levels between upstanding spikes and knife-edges of
rock. One of these, presumably, was topped by the monkey's
head. I could see nothing like it from here, but did not expect to. The point of view was the thing. A rock which
looked like a monkey's head to a man facing east could look
like the pope's nose of a plucked bird to a man facing south-
west. But it was there somewhere, and the only thing I could
do was to start at the seaward end of the turf and work my
way inland until I caught it, as Peter had, against the eastern
sky. The more I looked at the headland, the less I liked the
idea of it, but that clearly was what I had to do. Meanwhile I
thought that when I did attempt the headland, I would leave
my car somewhere south-west of it and come at it on foot
from that side, even perhaps, if the tide was right, along the
beach under the sea-wall. I could then, when I had done
whatever I found to do, drive back westwards and take the
turning I had just emerged from to get myself back to the
high ground, and so to town. Unless Claudio was by then on
the western headland itself, that should get me there unseen.
If I made the attempt in near darkness, as I had a mind to
do, it would also mean that even my headlights would hardly
be visible from the head of the bay before I was able to turn
them off and leave the car standing. And if I had to do the
thing at all, that was the only even remotely sensible way of
doing it.

I had now seen all I wanted to see, and had, I hoped, been
seen myself. But Claudio, wherever he was, could hardly
have seen the car, which was hidden under the sea-wall, and

I decided to show the flag nearer the enemy's camp. While I was about it, I might perhaps show a spurious interest in the next bay eastward, which might suggest to him, even if he had made up his own mind, that I was still uncertain of the real centre of interest. I got down off the wall, cleared a fresh deposit of salt from the glass of the car and drove on eastward. I went slowly, not so slowly as to be obviously trailing my coat, but slowly enough to suggest, perhaps, an uncertain frame of mind, as well as giving him a chance to get a good look at the car. This was the hotel, all right. It stood in what looked like an old hamlet, though even here there was a sprinkle of new houses, and a fair-sized road turned off right-handed almost next to it. That might for all I knew be the direct road back to town, but it was one I was in any case unlikely to use going either way. I drove on past the eastern headland and found the road setting into a curve following, presumably, the head of the next bay. There was a car parked on the side of the road near the centre of the curve, but it was not a grey Morris, and as I got closer I saw a bunch of figures, a family party by the look of it and a dog with them, on the wide stretch of turf which here led down to the beach. I had no idea what they were doing, except perhaps exercising the dog, but they were company at least, and with the houses on the landward side of the road fewer and further between, as they were here, I was glad of all the company I could get. I stopped my car not far from theirs and like them walked out over the turf to have, at least to all appearances, a considering look at the bay. I spent a few minutes on this exercise and then went back to my car. I had half a mind to turn and drive back the way I had come. I was not sure this was very good tactics, but I had done all I wanted, and the light was going with disconcerting speed, and my one idea now was to leave this bleak coast and get

back to the security of the town and the comfort of the hotel. I had started the engine and was on the point of swinging the car when my driving mirror picked up a car coming
up behind me from the west. It was a grey Minor. I know
now, looking back, that what I should have done was to turn
the engine off and stay where I was, in the company of the
other car and within sight of its owners still star-scattered on
the turf to seaward. If I had done that, all Claudio could
have done was simply to drive past. He could have confirmed his identification of me and my car, which was very
probably what he had come out to do, but I wanted him to
do this in any case, and there was nothing else he could have
done. Instead, while he was still a hundred yards or more behind, I pulled the car out onto the road and headed east-
wards. The grey Minor followed me, but showed no sign of
trying to catch up with me.

I cannot to this day swear that Claudio was in the grey
Minor. For all I know, it may not even have been a hire-car.
I never got a sight of its number plate, to see if there was an
H on it. But I assumed, almost certainly correctly, that it was
Claudio on the road behind me, and I did not know what
was the best thing to do. I could follow the coast-road indefinitely until he had seen me off his ground and gave up the
pursuit, but this would land me God knows where and leave
me to grope my way home in darkness through the network
of the island roads, which looked bad enough
on the map and were even more confusing on the ground.
Or I could do what I ought to have done to start with, stop
the car somewhere where I was sure of an audience, let him
drive past and then turn and head for home by roads I had
at least explored by daylight. Or I could find what looked a
suitable right-hand turning and take it, trusting that all the

bigger roads at least headed for the town and leaving Claudio again to follow me until he got tired of it.

I do not know what there was about Claudio that made me take so many wrong decisions in my dealings with him. I think it was not so much a matter of underestimating my opponent as of losing patience with him. There was something so lunatic in his persistence that I was tempted to force the pace and lost control of the game doing so. It happens, of course, in all sorts of contests between man and man, from boxing to chess, and exasperation is always the root of disaster. I expect Goliath felt a surge of exasperation as the first smooth stone from the brook sang past his head, and dropped his guard once too often. I think if I had come to a brightly lit garage, I should have turned in for unwanted petrol, or if Claudio had shown any sign of doing anything but driving steadily a hundred yards behind me, I might have hung on a bit longer. As it was, I felt that he was simply driving me further and further out of my way and did not see why the hell I should let him, and when I came to a reasonable-looking turn off to the right, I took it.

I could not see what Claudio's reaction was, because I had lost sight of him from the moment I turned, but it did not take me long to realise that I had taken a wrong turning. The road narrowed almost at once, and began to climb quite steeply between the high turf banks which seemed to be the standard fencing on the island. It was winding, too, and getting rougher, and there seemed to be no houses anywhere, only the occasional field-gate in the bank. I think I knew what was going to happen before it actually did, but it happened soon enough. The road, now no more than a lane, forked suddenly, but the forks were both closed by field-gates. There was a triangle of grass between the banks, but no way ahead. I had run myself into a dead end, and a lonely one at that, and I had a picture of Claudio, with his gun warm in his pocket, following up behind me to obtain the confidential interview he had long sought. The place was private enough, but I could hardly expect an island Daphnis and Chloe to appear here in search of solitude, as my Stonham couple had, or not, unless they were very desperate, in these conditions.

I think in a way it was exasperation that got me out of the trap as much as it was exasperation that had landed me in it. I did the fool thing again, but this time it paid off. It was all but fully dark now, and I could have abandoned my car and disappeared into the darkness, leaving Claudio little chance of finding me, but then he could have sat out the situation indefinitely in his car, leaving me equally little chance of getting mine back onto the road again, let alone of finding my way home. I did not know where he was at the moment. I did not even know whether he had followed me up my side-turning from the coast-road. But I was damned if I was going to wait here to find out. I backed and turned the car furiously in the triangular space available and set off down the lane again. I had still not put my lights on, but I could see a glimmer of grey sky between the dark banks, and I was in no danger of losing my way. I must have been half-way down to the coast-road when I saw the side-lights of a car coming slowing up the lane to meet me. Claudio knew the ground and was in no hurry. He also presumably wanted to take me as far as possible by surprise. I did not calculate the thing at all. I reckoned there was just enough room between the banks for two small cars to pass each other, and I trusted to Claudio, when it came to the crunch, to do the instinctive thing. I waited until he was perhaps thirty yards from me in a mercifully straight stretch of lane, and then I put my headlights full on and drove straight down at him. For a moment or two I thought he was going to meet me head-on, and I could not have stopped my car if I had wanted to, not on that slope. Then at the last moment he did what I hoped he would, and what almost anyone would have. He stepped on his brakes and pulled in hard against the bank on his side. I took a tight grip on the wheel, aimed at the gap between the off-side of the Minor and the bank on my side, and kept going.

There cannot have been more than inches between the cars, and for several yards my near-side brushed the grass of the bank, but I made it. Already the lane was opening up to its deceptively impressive width where it joined the road, and a moment later my lights picked up the tarmac of the road and the sea-wall beyond it. I braked, swung left, and drove as fast as I dared south-westwards. It would take Claudio some time to extricate himself from the lane, and I did not think he would follow me again that evening, but I was taking no chances. It was only when I was through the cutting at the landward end of the headland that I let the pace down, looking for the turning I had come out of what now seemed a very long time ago. I found it, turned into it with a feeling of almost nonsensical relief and set off steadily for the higher ground. It was only then it occurred to me that I had not seen Claudio at all. For the first time I had had him face to face, caught in the white light of my headlamps, and I had not even looked at him. My concentration had been entirely on the gap I had had to get through. I had no doubt this had been wise in the circumstances, but it struck me as a pity, all the same.

Whether it was that the mere thought of Claudio was having its usual effect on me, or whether I was just over-relaxed, it was now that I really lost my way. I had of course driven down the hill by daylight, simply aiming for the sea. Now it was dark and I had the whole width of the island, such as it was, ahead of me, and all my headlights picked up was that damned intricate tangle of small island roads. Even the names on the sign-posts meant nothing to me. I had to ask my way three times, and even so must have steered a wildly erratic course to town. When at last I pulled up outside the hotel, the dining-room windows were aglow with tastefully subdued pinkish lighting, and I could see my fellow-guests already at dinner. I went straight up to my room, picked up the telephone receiver and asked for Lisa's room. I let the bell ring for quite a time, but there was no reply. I supposed she must be dining, and tidied myself as best I could before going down to do the same.

The dining-room was barely half full, and before I had even let the head waiter install me at a small table, I had already seen that Lisa was not there. There seemed to be nothing I could do, and I was suddenly desperately hungry. I simply sat down, ordered myself what looked like a promising dinner and a half-bottle of wine to go with it, and hoped for the best. I suppose I must have been concentrating unduly on the soup, which was very good, because I suddenly looked up and saw her, also in the care of the head waiter, not a dozen yards from me. He was putting her at another small table, with only one table, and that empty, between us, She must have seen me at the same moment. For a second she stood stock still, and then rejected the chair he had pulled out for her, which had its back to me, and deliberately sat down on the other side of the table, facing me. She ordered her dinner with the utmost composure and then, when the man was gone, suddenly lifted her head and looked at me.

It is a shattering experience, when you are no longer young and have given up expecting it, or even perhaps want-

ing it, suddenly to know that you are of importance to someone. She gave me a smile of the purest pleasure, perhaps
tinged with relief, and I smiled back, pleased at her pleasure.
When the waiter brought her her first course, with a half-
bottle to match mine, she set about it with a determination
equal to my own, but every now and then, throughout the
meal, we caught each other's eye and smiled, and once
before she drank she lifted her glass in my direction and I
lifted mine in hers. We were a dozen yards apart and unable
to say a word to each other, a little distracted but both in
good appetite, and mentally very much tête-à-tête. And so
we dined.

153

CHAPTER 14.

The wind roared round the hotel louder than ever, but when I opened the door of my room, the air had the bottled timeless feel of hotel corridors at night. I locked the door behind me and kept the key in my hand. I had the Colt in the right-hand pocket of my raincoat and the key of Lisa's car in my trouser pocket. I had left her the key of the Triumph, but hoped she would not use it. I did not take the lift, but padded down the thickly carpeted stairs in the total silence and the yellow night lighting. The night-porter was in his box, but I had primed him the evening before with some story of bird-watching at first light. I do not know whether he believed me, but I do not suppose it bothered him. Whatever I went out for at that time of the morning in that weather, it was bound to be daft and unlikely to be criminal. He took my key and gave me in exchange a smile with a dash of pity in it. Then he went back to his book. It was a paper-back, but very solid. I could not see the title, but his face had the slightly glazed determination of a man reading Tolstoi. I went out through the revolving glass doors into the damp moving air and the faint street-lighting of the sea-front. The wind was still hitting the far side of the island, but even here the sea swell moaned and thumped under the sea-wall. The tide must have been rising when I had seen it in the afternoon, and now it was nearly full high again.

I unlocked the grey Minor and settled myself in the driving seat, and despite the damp air, the engine started first go. I knew why that was. It was because Lisa had been out looking for me during the evening. She had not found me, and had got in after I had. We had not spoken in the public parts of the hotel after dinner, but we had spoken briefly on the telephone, and then I had gone along to her room. I had to get the gun and exchange car-keys with her, and that was about all we had done. After the warm, unspoken communicativeness of the dining-room, she had been abrupt and curiously on the defensive when she had met me face to face in her room, and I had not pressed her. Only now in the last hours of the night I found that she was very much in my mind, but only at the back of it. The front of my mind was too much occupied with other things.

I had done a lot of work on the map before I went to bed, and I did not think I could lose my way this time, even in full darkness. In any case, I had given myself plenty of time, and when all was said, the distances involved were tiny. I planned to head direct for the south-west corner of the island, where there was a lighthouse on an outlying reef, as God knows there should be, marking the western extremity of this lethal stumbling block in what must be much frequented waters. The whole southern side of the island had high cliffs and deep-water bays, quite different from that flat, sea-scoured coast in the north, and the main road westward from the town followed a line well back from the sea and mostly, as far as I could tell from the map, out of sight of it. I had taken off a large-scale sketch map of the road, in particular noting the place-names on each side of it, so that I should be able to identify and reject the various side-roads I did not want to follow. Towards the south-west corner of the island the land fell sharply and levelled out, and I ought to be able to see the flash of the lighthouse well before I got there. Once there, I had only to turn sharply to the north-east and follow the coast-road, and sooner or later I must come to my headland, as I wanted to, from its western side. But before I got there I meant to park the car, perhaps in the side-road I had come out of the day before, and do the rest of the journey on foot.

The wind was as strong as ever, perhaps even stronger, but the cloud had broken, so that there were occasional glimpses of a dying moon far down in the west. For the rest I had a small pocket torch, but would not use it unless I had to. As things now were, I thought Claudio was capable of scanning the headland for lights at intervals during the night, though I did not think that even he would be ready to spend the night there. My purpose, of course, was to see that damned monkey's head against the first light in the east, as Peter had seen it twenty years before, and to be off the head-land and back to my car before there was any real daylight on the ground. The fact that the sky was clearing should help, but that was about the best I could make of it. Lisa had left the car facing north, but I swung round in the width of the deserted sea-front and headed west through the gusty, empty streets of the town.

I drove slowly and with a sort of febrile carefulness, watching every turning and road junction as I came to it and checking it off on the precise mental picture I had of the sketch map lying on the empty seat beside me. On the two or three occasions I found myself in any degree of doubt, I stopped and studied both the map and the ground until I was satisfied. I could not have done this in daylight, with the roads full of traffic, but perhaps in daylight I should not have needed to. I was in something of the frame of mind of a man stalking a dangerous quarry, hell-bent on doing it without mishap and not jangling his nerves before he need. The wind

156

almost stopped the car as I came over the hump of the high ground, and even when I could see the flash of the lighthouse ahead and below me, I had to force my way steadily in third gear as if I had been driving up-hill. Nevertheless, I completed the first part of my drive without trouble, and it was only when I had swung north-eastward and taken the wind on my near side that I wondered whether I had been wise after all to leave myself so much of the coast-road to negotiate before I got to the scene of action. The tarmac was sticky with salt water and littered with torn seaweed and fair-sized pebbles, and the air so full of spray that I had to use the windscreen wipers continuously, and every now and then the washers to clear the accumulated drift of salt on the glass.

The road edged steadily nearer to the sea until I found myself driving, as I had the day before with the sea-wall only yards from the side of the car, and it was then I got my first real fright. Suddenly, but with a sort of ponderous slowness, an enormous white column reared up not twenty yards ahead of me, and hung there for a split second in the white glare of the head-lights, and then disintegrated in a drift of white smoke across the whole width of the road. For a moment my foot eased on the accelerator and I made to swing the car to the right, but I knew that would not do, and forced the car steadily forward again. The tide must be at full high, and the bigger waves were breaking on the sea-wall itself, but I did not think that even if this happened immediately beside me it could do me any real harm. My only anxiety was that the wet drift might find its way to the plugs or the distributor and cut out the engine, but it was coming from the side, not from ahead, and I thought that if I kept the engine turning fast and the car moving steadily but slowly, this was not likely. I put the engine in third, and

157

sometimes even in second, for the dangerous stretches, and although before I had finished my drive I saw the sea several times break across the road ahead, I was never caught in the full force of the explosion.

What it would be like in these conditions on the headland itself, if and when I got there, I did not like to think, but I took comfort in the thought that, even if I was mad enough to go there, Claudio with any luck would not be, and indeed would probably reckon it unnecessary. I had constantly to remind myself that he could not possibly have any idea of the sort of clue I had to follow. Almost inevitably he would be thinking in terms of cross-bearings or distances paced out from fixed points on the ground, any of which would need at least a reasonable amount of daylight. I reckoned he had probably forgotten, as I had myself until I had read Peter's letter, the exact timing of daybreak, on that morning twenty years ago, relative to our various movements on or near the beach, and the fact that Peter had cached the box and marked down the hiding-place in near darkness had probably not occurred to him. Meanwhile, I pushed on along the big curves of the coast-road, sometimes nearer than I liked to that raging sea, sometimes at a more comfortable distance from it, until I knew I must be getting near the end of my drive. I might well, in these conditions, miss the right-hand turning I was looking for, but I did not think my head-lights could fail to pick up, well before I got there, that grisly white-walled house above the cutting in the base of the headland itself, and once I saw that I should know I had come far enough. I might, in fact, already have come too far, but if so, I had only to manoeuvre the car round in the width of the road and drive back slowly until I found my turning.

When it came to the point, I saw the house and my turning at almost the same moment, or at least from almost the same spot. My head-lights picked up a white gleam some way ahead, and I brought my speed, already slow enough, down to a crawl, peering through the smeared glass and trying to get a clearer view. Already the curve of the road had swung my lights leftwards off the house, if it was the house, and I thought if I could swing the car a little to the right in the width of the road, I might pick it up again. I brought my eyes back to the road immediately ahead, and found a good-sized side-road opening up on my right hand only a few yards ahead. It was as I remembered it, flat and open and unmarked, and I could easily have driven past it, but here was what looked like the right turning, and there ahead was what looked like the house, and I thought the odds against mere coincidence were too long. I swung the car into the turning and drove slowly, with the wind for the first time behind me, looking for somewhere to leave the car. The further I drove, the more walking I should have to do, but against this I did not want the car, if daylight came to it before I did, to be too obvious from the coast-road. I also thought it prudent, even facing away from the sea, to leave it clear of the worst of the spindrift blowing in across the flat ground from the bedlam of breaking water on the other side of the sea-wall. I had not gone more than forty or fifty yards when the road swung left a little and a thin hedge of tamarisk came up on its left-hand side. The wiry, tufted plants lashed about and leant sideways in the wind, but they endured it. I thought they were probably the only plants that could grow to any size in this salt-drenched soil and the perennial sea-winds. At any rate, there they were, and I pulled the car as close in under them as I could get it and stopped.

I had already decided not to leave my lights on. Daylight was at least on the way, and such traffic as there was in these conditions would be moving slowly. The risk of a collision or

a police summons was negligible compared with the risk that
Claudio, perhaps out on a dawn patrol, would see the rear-
lights from the coast-road as he drove past the turning. Of
course it was not the car he would be expecting to find, but
it was a hire-car. Parked and empty at this place and time
and in these conditions, it would be bound to stink in his
nostrils if once he got a sight of it. I turned off everything
and checked the lock on the near-side door. Once more, as I
had the day before, I buttoned my raincoat to the neck and
pulled my hat tight down on my head. I patted the gun in
my right-hand pocket and the torch in my left. Then I
opened the door and got out. This time the wind, coming
from behind, nearly dragged the door out of my hand, and,
in fact, dragged me almost bodily out of the car with the
swinging door. I managed just in time to stop the door slamming back on its hinges, manoeuvred round it until my
weight was behind it and then forced it shut and locked it. I
put the key carefully into my trouser pocket, bowed my
head into that lunatic wind and started off back the way I
had come, making for the coast-road.

I had expected to get wet, and was dressed for it, but I
had not allowed for the saltness of the wetting. I thought by
the time I got home my raincoat would have to be soaked in
a fresh-water bath before it could be dried. Along the whole
stretch of coast-road between the side turning and the cutting the spray blew over me in clouds I could not see but felt
in their various degrees of violence and wetness. Even under
the partial shelter of the sea-wall, the wind was perpetually
driving me sideways, so that I went forward in a sort of staggering zigzag, and even on the tarmac of the road the shift-
ing, slippery debris of the storm made the going uncertain.
By the time I got into the shelter of the cutting I felt as tired

as if I had swum the distance, and I still had not met the full force of the wind.

Opposite me, as I crouched under the seaward side of the cutting, the white house stood up greyly in the howling darkness, as impersonal as a rock. I could make out no detail, but there were certainly no lights. I suppose the inhabitants were used to these conditions and had got their heads well under the bedding. With the spray no longer blowing into my eyes, and my eyes themselves adjusted to the darkness as far as they ever would be, I could see a fair amount of detail near at hand but little at any distance. The driving water-vapour seemed to carry a certain light of its own, as thick fogs do, but to the straining eye it was more opaque than mere darkness. The moon was long since down, and only a few stars showed fleetingly in gaps of the racing cloud bank. Even so, I reckoned that when the first grey showed in the sky eastward, I should be able to see it, but I did not think that could happen for half-an-hour or so yet. In the meantime I had to get out as near to the seaward end of the headland as I could and wait for it.

I got up and walked back to the western side of the cutting and then, as the wind leapt on me again, turned full into it and set out across the turf slope of the headland. I was wearing heavy boots with deep-cut treads, but even so I found the going damnably slippery. Where the turf was smooth, it was scurfed with wet salt, and between the smooth stretches the rock broke out of it at every angle. I went forward bent almost double, partly to shield my mouth and nostrils from the direct blast of the wind and partly to make sure of the ground before I put a foot down. If I had had something to protect my hands, I think I should have got down on all fours and crawled, but since it was still not cold, I had not thought of gloves. If I turned my head and

161

looked up, I could just make out the jagged central spine
closing in above me on my right as the breaking sea closed in
below me on my left, but with the wind blowing as it was
straight along the line of the headland I knew I should get no
more shelter from it whichever side I was on. After a bit the
turf broken by occasional rocky outcrops gave way to more
continuous rock, though even here there were still strips and
pockets of turf wherever the fissured rock gave it a foothold.
To my surprise I suddenly found the going easier. Even on
the wet rock my boots took a better grip than they had on
the turf, and with the rocks rising round me at least I had
something for my hands to hold on to. I could even set my
back against a rock and rest occasionally, whereas out on the
open turf there was no escape anywhere from the relentless
pressure of the wind. But the spray was getting thicker every
minute as the headland narrowed to the point where it met
the direct onset of the sea. I was still some way from actual
breaking water, but I felt as wet as if I was already in it.

I clambered over the rocks in that bedlam of savage wind
and blown water until there seemed to be no more turf anywhere under my groping feet and nothing but a slope of
streaming rock between me and the breaking surf. Then at
last I steadied myself, put a rock between me and the wind,
and turned and looked back. For all the state I was in, I felt
a surge of real satisfaction at what I saw, and knew that the
worst was over. The headland had narrowed and dropped
until I was now virtually on the central spine itself. From
here I could make my way inland along the other side of the
headland, leaving the high rocks on my right hand. This was
the way Peter had come all those years ago. He had been
moving, as I should be, roughly eastward, and when he had
seen the grey light in the eastern sky, he had seen it almost
ahead, with the ragged tops of the central spine of rock out-

lined against it. That was when he had seen the monkey's head, and that was where I could surely see it too, given time and an at least intermittently clear sky to eastward. And already, as I looked, I knew that the eastern sky was lightening. Within almost a matter of minutes, I thought, I could be crouching with my long-bladed knife in my hand, probing the turf at the foot of the rock for the steel box Peter had left there nine inches down. All I needed was a little time, and a little luck, and a little more light in the east. I stood there, with the wind and spray savaging my back, taking my time, and hoping for luck, and waiting for the light. I waited until I could see, even from here, the high tops of the rock in reasonably clear outline against the clearer patches of sky. Then I left my rock, turning myself to face slightly left, and began my long clamber back towards the land.

So far as making my way went, it was incomparably easier than the outward climb to the point. I now had the wind behind me, and I was, in general, going up rather than down, which is always the safer direction over bad going. Even so, I went slower than ever, because merely making my way was now a secondary consideration. My sole purpose was to observe. When I moved, I moved only to change my point of view, and I did it only a yard or two at a time. Each time I stood I observed afresh the whole visible range of rocks above me, and with the light still as faint as it was, and the cloud cover constantly changing, I often had to wait for quite a time until I was satisfied with my observation. From what Peter had written, he had been well up onto the turf slope before he had found his place, but that did not mean that the monkey's head could be seen only from there. I was looking for it yard by yard almost from the edge of the breaking sea, but I came at last onto the turf slope, and I still had not seen it.

It was lighter on the ground now, not only in the sky. I still could not see far, but I could see more than I could when I started on my climb back. On this side of the headland, I suppose because it was the leeside in the prevailing westerly winds, there was more turf than on the other, and it reached further seaward. I seemed to be in a sort of long corridor, turfed underfoot, with the central rock-spine on my right and a lesser line of rock running parallel with it on my left. This would be the rock which, as I had seen from the head of the bay, on its outer side fell sheer almost to the level of the beach. I had no wish to investigate it and did not need to. It was topped with a continuous jagged knife-edge, not broken into separate crags and columns as the central spine was, and there could be no monkey's head there. It was not even, on my side, very high, and the turf sloped up from under it to the base of the higher rocks on the right. It occurred to me that it would not screen me, given visibility enough, from observation from across the bay. If the sky continued to clear, and the light grew as it was growing at the moment, I must be off this side of the headland before Claudio gave it his morning once-over. In the meantime, it was the crags in the centre that concerned me, and I went up the turf slope, yard by yard, stopping and observing, and moving on and stopping, and still I could not see anything remotely like the monkey's head of Peter's sketch.

I do not know how long I went on before I gave it up. I know I doubled back more than once, and repeated the process of observation over again, and all the time the light was growing, until I knew I must not stay on the headland any longer. The light was still no more than a grey dusk, but the visibility was certainly lengthening, and as the tide fell, the curtains of flying spray no longer blanketed the headland so continuously, or reached so far up it. I worked my way down to the bottom of the spine for the last time, and this time rounded it and went back landwards, as I had first come out, on its south-eastern side. I was fairly certain by now that not only was the tide falling, the wind itself was less violent than it had been. The gale might blow itself out by morning, and so far as I was concerned it was welcome to. The sea was frightening enough in its proper place, without getting at me from over the sea-wall.

There were still no lights in the white house, and no cars on the road. I was very tired now, and cold, and above all hungry, but I made good time back to the car. It stood where I had left it under the threshing tamarisks, and this time I raked the whole inside with my torch before I so much as tried the door. There was no one in the car, and when I tried the door, I found it still locked. I took off my salt-sodden raincoat and rolled it into a bundle and dropped it on the floor of the car between the front and rear seats. My clothes under it were damp enough, but I hoped most of the salt would have stayed on the raincoat. I could get the driving seat dry by the time I had to, but did not want to have to wash the salt out of it first. The car started obediently, and I switched the lights on and headed for town.

One thing apart, it had been a successful operation. I had outmanoeuvred the enemy, and made my reconnaissance in my chosen conditions, and come and gone unseen, which was satisfactory as far as it went. Only I had not found what I was looking for, and I had no idea now where it could be.

165

CHAPTER 15.

Lisa said, "You're sure you've got the right headland?"

"Claudio agrees with me about the bay," I said, "and we know which side of the bay Peter came ashore. It's got to be right."

"Could you have seen the monkey's head and not recognised it—seen it from a slightly different angle, say?"

I thought about this. I said, "Of course I can't swear I ever got onto the exact spot where Peter was when he saw it. But I must at least once, probably more than once, have got very near it, near enough for an object seen at that distance to look almost exactly the same. And I tell you, I never saw anything like it. I never even saw anything that seemed to call for a second look. I never had even a moment's hope."

"What about the light—the degree of light, or the angle of light? Any possible difference there?"

"When Peter made his observation, I was still in the sea, tied to that damned raft. I wasn't worrying much about the light. But the time of year's much the same, and Peter said he could see only about twenty yards, which also sounds right. As for angle, it's not a matter of a pin-point of light at one precise place. Once it comes, the light diffuses itself over quite a wide stretch of sky. Peter may have had a clearer sky than I had, and better visibility generally because the tide was lower than it was this morning, and there'd have been less spray. Less wind to carry it, even. Conditions at the time of the wreck can't have been as bad as they were today, or I don't think we'd have reached land at all. We'd have foundered out at sea, or at least been dismasted, and the mast was still there when we struck. But I can't really believe there was all that difference. No, it's nothing like that, not a question of degree. There's something fundamentally wrong somewhere. Either I didn't look in the right place, or the damned thing's no longer there—the monkey's head I mean, not the box. But of course it must be—it would have been a built-in part of the island." I looked at her and she looked at me. "Human error," I said, "either Peter's or mine."

She said, "I don't believe it was Peter's. It meant too much to him."

I nodded and shrugged. "Neither do I. All right then, mine. I'll just have to look again."

She said, "By daylight," and I looked back at her for a moment, and then I nodded again.

"All right," I said, "by daylight."

She was still looking at me, and now she smiled, with her mouth but hardly at all with her eyes. "And this time," she said, "I'm coming too."

For a few seconds I stared back at her, and then, I think rather to her surprise, I nodded. "All right," I said. It had not taken me long to make up my mind. I knew what we had in hand, and I knew that an extra person on the ground, and a competent one at that, could make all the difference, especially when their presence would not be suspected by the enemy. Left to myself, I think I would have given the thing up there and then. I knew, as I had just told Lisa, that there was something fundamentally wrong somewhere, either in Peter's directions or else in my understanding of them. I even considered the possibility of cornering Claudio in some place where he would be harmless, perhaps in his room at the hotel, and telling him exactly how matters stood. But there was another factor in it too. I was determined to prove that my carefully planned and perfectly executed reconnaissance had not failed through any fault of mine. To prove it, I suppose, primarily to Lisa, who with her total faith in Peter would not accept it without further and conclusive demonstration. Beyond Lisa, I was determined to prove it to Claudio too. It would do me no good to give the thing up if I was going to be haunted for the rest of my life by an obsessed Claudio. I had to go on the headland again, and in full daylight, and I knew from what I had already seen of it that I could not do that without bringing Claudio on the spot at the double. It was essential, if I was to handle him successfully, or if possible avoid him altogether, to have warning of his approach, and I could not conduct a conclusive search for the monkey's head and watch for him at the same time. That was where Lisa would come in. Suitably posted, she could warn me of his approach well before he arrived, and that could make the difference between success and failure, possibly even between life and death. I had to go, and I had to have her with me. It was simply a matter of working out a plan and getting her to agree to it. I told her, not perhaps exactly what my reasons were, but what we had to do, and we got down to the discussion of details.

But I was not going to do any more that day. I had had a very short night's sleep, and I had been tired and hungry and wet and apprehensive, and now that I was warm and dry and fed, all this was coming back at me in a natural lassitude. The Establishment had been in the habit of getting you on the active strength and under orders a good forty-eight hours before you were actually needed, and the general view was that, whatever they said, their real object was to get you fresh, rather as international footballers are frowned upon if seen in the local night-clubs or brothels on the eve of an important match. I was not subject to orders now, but I knew enough not to tackle Claudio openly on his home ground feeling in any degree below par. And if the wind dropped in the meantime, so much the better. There was one small piece of shopping to do, which Lisa said she would do that afternoon. There was only one point of detail left undecided, the actual position of Lisa's look-out, but this could only be decided on the ground. So we fixed the operation for about half-tide next day, and I had an early lunch and went without apology to bed.

I was awakened by the telephone on the bedside table. I knew that there was only one person who would telephone my room, and I took time to get my head reasonably clear before I spoke to her. I noticed, in the meantime, that the weather had changed outside, and there was sunshine behind the drawn curtains. Then I picked up the receiver and gave the room number. She said, "Ben? You've had a good sleep. Feel better?"

"I feel fine," I said. "Did you get what you wanted?" What she had wanted was a whistle, an ordinary whistle as worn by referees and boy scouts, though I had never actually heard a boy scout blowing one.

"Yes," she said. "Very penetrating and startling." She hesitated for a moment. Then she said, "I've found my place, too."

I did not like this. I admitted the desirability of fixing the place in advance, but I still did not like it. I said, "You mean you've been on the ground?"

Something of my disapproval must have got into my voice, because she said, "Yes, but not right on, and only for a moment or two. I'm sure there's no harm done."

There was no point in arguing or asking for details. What

was done was done. If the enemy had profited by it, we should know soon enough. I said, "All right. Where is it?"

"Right up on top of the rocks, almost at the base of the headland, quite near the road. I didn't go up there, of course, I merely saw it from below. But there's a way up I can manage, and a hollow between two crags where I ought to be able to lie low enough and still get a view."

"All right," I said. "Good. You used your own car, of course?"

She said, "Of course," a little abruptly. "You said he hadn't seen it."

"No," I said. "No, I don't think he can have. But better not meet in the meantime, just in case. I'll see you at dinner, Lisa, but no more. And tomorrow we leave independently at the agreed time. All right?"

"All right," she said. She still sounded a little miffed. "And if you see my head against the sky when you're looking for the monkey's head, don't let it confuse you."

I said, "I shouldn't think of making such an elementary mistake."

"Well, good," she said. "Till tomorrow, then." I did not see her, in fact, at dinner. I did not see her again, or even hear her voice, until the thing was practically all over.

She left half-an-hour ahead of me, driving the grey Minor. I drove the Triumph, following the same route. Well before I got to the coast-road I could see the Minor on the road ahead of me, parked under the tamarisk hedge where I had parked it in the small hours of the day before, but facing in the other direction. I drove past it to the coast-road and then, as I turned north-eastward, turned to look back at it. It was visible, of course, if you looked for it, but it did not stand out at all. I doubted if anyone driving along the coast-road would see it unless they had a special reason for looking. It was a bright day, with isolated clouds driving before a wind that, though still from the north-west, was not much more than a stiff breeze. I stopped the car for a moment and went to the sea-wall to have a look at the sea. It had nothing like the fury of the day before, but it was still formidable. There was a huge round swell rolling in from God knows how many miles of open sea still labouring under the after-effects of the storm, and with the wind still behind it, it was breaking thunderously on the foot of the stone beach and the rocks of the headland. Also, it was less far down than I had expected. Either I had got the timing wrong, or the wind and swell together were counteracting the pull of the tide. Not that that should matter. It was not the sea I was concerned with, and there were no curtains of flying spray to restrict visibility. I got back into the car and drove on until I was almost at the base of the headland. Then I simply pulled the car off the road onto the turf by the sea-wall and stopped. I locked it and put the key in my pocket, but I made no attempt to conceal it. Concealment was not part of my strategy today, and it would only have wasted vital time. I walked straight along the road and up onto the turf of the headland. Lisa, for whom concealment was vital, would have walked along the top of the beach under the sea-wall and got up onto the headland from under its south-western side. I allowed myself one quick glance at the crags near the base of the headland, but could see no sign of her. That was as it should be. I had not the slightest doubt she was there somewhere, and had seen me.

I had approached the headland from the south-west to give myself as much time as possible before my movements were seen from across the bay, but once there I was concerned only with speed. I went out along the north-eastern side, with the central spine on my left, because that was

171

where I had to renew my search. I did not even go anything like to the seaward end. I went down to the limit of the continuous turf, already with my eyes on the rocks above me, and then turned and started slowly back, surveying the crests of rock foot by foot. I knew almost from the start that it was no good. I knew that if the damned monkey's head had been there, anywhere, against the sky, I should have seen it the day before, and should be seeing it now. I still went on looking. I was looking up so intently that when I came to a jumble of small rocks in the turf, I missed my footing and fell. I did not fall hard. I merely stumbled and came down on my hands and knees.

It was then that I saw, for the first time but quite unmistakably, the monkey's head. I saw it then because it was not outlined against the sky over my head, but outlined against the turf not a couple of feet from my down-turned face. I say, there was no mistaking it. It was exactly as Peter had sketched it, and even lay at the same angle. It was half sunk in the turf and had no neck. Above and behind it there was a drift of jumbled rocks of all sizes, some of them more than man-size. The drift was piled up against the base of a single large rock running up perhaps ten feet to a flat, splintered top. Even from here I could see that by comparison with the higher crags the top was still only partially weathered.

There was no arguing the thing at all. The facts were written large over the whole picture. There had indeed been a high column of rock standing above the turf, and it had indeed been topped by the monkey's head, but at some moment in the last twenty years the rock had fallen. I suppose it had been undercut by weathering near its base. I knew where the base of the rock under the monkey's head had been, and I had no doubt that the box was still there under the turf. But on top of it, and spread out in three directions

172

round it, there was this huge, immovable jumble of broken rock. There must have been tons of it and, as I say, for all practicable purposes immovable. A bulldozer could have shifted it, but you could not get a bulldozer here. Explosive would have shifted it, but only at the quite certain price of destroying the box as well. But above all there was the question of secrecy. In my concentration on Claudio it had been easy for me to forget the legal aspects of what I was trying to do. The fact remained that to take possession of the box, whether Claudio did it or I did, was almost certainly an illegal act, and to be worth doing had to be done in secrecy or not at all. To shift this amount of rock from where it was, was difficult enough. To shift it secretly, was out of the question. The thing was unanswerable. There was no need to postulate any human interference. As Peter himself had said, the headland was, in terms of geological time, steadily disintegrating, and even in geological time the moment must be reached when a particular piece of rock yields to the forces against it—and falls. Some time in the last twenty years that moment had been reached, and there was nothing I or anyone else could do about it.

CHAPTER 16.

I got slowly to my feet. There was nothing to do now but go, and I had still had no whistle signal from Lisa to show that Claudio was on the way. I took one last look round the place, and as I looked seaward saw, twenty or thirty yards from me, a hat. It showed for a moment over the top of a rock and disappeared again, but I knew whose hat it was. I even fancied it was slightly on one side. Not for the first time, but now for the last, Claudio had anticipated me and had taken me in the rear. Lisa had not seen him because he had already been there, out near the end of the headland, when she had arrived. For that matter, he probably had not seen her either. Now he was moving up to take me by surprise, perhaps even hoping to catch me in the act of unearthing what he had wanted all these years. I knew now that there was nothing for us to fight about, but I also knew that I did not want, of all places, to confront him with the fact here. I dropped to my knees again and looked for a way of escape.

The straight line was up the rising corridor of turf, but that would bring me into full view long before I got to the top, and I had not the slightest doubt that when he saw me Claudio would shoot at once. He would see me apparently escaping with the thing in my pocket, and he would shoot, and I did not for a moment suppose that he would miss. I could not go seaward, because that was where Claudio was, and on my right there was only the wall of broken rock which, even if I could climb it, would leave me even more of a sitting target. There was nothing for it but to go left and try to find a way landward between the sea and the rock wall on that side. This was the one part of the headland I had sworn to avoid at all costs, but now I had no choice. I crawled across to the low wall of rock, looked back, could not see Claudio anywhere, and then stood up and peered over.

There was hope here, not much, but some. The sea was rolling ponderously at regular intervals over the jumble of rocks at the foot of the wall, but above the water, and not far below me as I looked down at it, a single ledge ran the length of the rock face, climbing landward on a line roughly parallel with its top. It was a natural ledge, some trick of the upended strata of hard rock that formed the headland, but it looked negotiable. The rock might well be undercut below it, but did not overhang above it, and I thought it should be possible, if I flattened myself against the rock face, to get my feet onto it with my centre of gravity still inshore of my feet. What happened to the ledge at its upper end I could not see from here, but at least it offered a way of escape to a point nearer the land, and above all it was out of sight from where Claudio now was. He would find it, of course, sooner or later as he came up the slope of the headland. He might already know of its existence. But it might just give me a chance of escape before he caught me on it, and it was the only chance I had. I moved a few yards down the slope, partly to give myself more cover, but mainly because from there the rock face sloped decisively outward to the ledge, so that I should not so much drop onto it as slide down to it. I took one more look seaward, still saw no Claudio, and slithered feet first and face down over the edge of the rock. I hooked my hands onto the last sharp wrinkle of rock, let my feet down as far as they would go, took one deep breath and let myself slide.

It was, in fact, as I had judged it would be—a very short slide. My feet at full stretch cannot have been much more than a yard above the ledge, and landed on it before I had time to gather any speed. There seemed plenty of it for them to land on, too, and my slide was checked immediately and completely. For a moment I stayed there, spread-eagled with my face pressed against the wet face of the rock, simply getting my wits back. Then, without moving my body more than I could help, I turned my head and looked first down at my feet and then along the ledge as it climbed landwards. I still could not see its upper end, because after ten yards or so it seemed to turn around a shoulder of rock, but so far as I could see it it looked negotiable enough, and now every second counted. I turned my face to the wall again, arched my body so that I could just see down between it and the rock and began to shuffle sideways along the ledge.

I shall never know from what point Claudio was watching my progress, but he must certainly have been watching it closely from some point, and must equally certainly have known that my escape route was a dead end. At any rate, he delayed his intervention to the moment of greatest psychological impact, and with results which he clearly did not intend or even anticipate. Meanwhile I kept going steadily along the ledge, arms spread wide for possible finger-holds, body held just clear of the rock, face turned down to see my present and next foothold on the ledge, but never much beyond that. I wondered, of course, where Claudio was and what he was up to, but there was nothing I could do about him anyway, and the only thing that mattered was to keep going until I turned the shoulder and found a way back on to the base of the headland. I came to the shoulder at last, reached my left foot to the furthest point of the ledge I could see and slithered my body across the rock-face as my right foot followed it. Then I stopped dead, because there was nothing else I could do. The ledge did not turn the shoulder of the rock, it broke off short six inches beyond my left foot. From what I could see, it went on again about a yard further on and a few inches higher up, but in between there was a great vertical split in the rock, going right down to the present level of the sea, so that I could hear the water muttering and sucking at the bottom of it as the waves came and went. There was nothing I could do at all. If the ledge had been wider, so that I could face along it instead of having to take it sideways, I could have stepped across the gap with no trouble at all. I may be afraid of water, but there is nothing wrong with my head for heights. But of course there was no room for that. I could not turn myself to face along the ledge without overbalancing outwards and falling into the sea, and I could not reach sideways across the gap without overbalancing inwards and falling into the cleft. It was at that moment that Claudio spoke from somewhere above my head. He said, "Properly stuck, aren't you?"

I am not sure to this day exactly what happened after that, but I must have reacted sharply in some way which my physical circumstances did not permit. I only know that first one foot and then the other slipped off the ledge, dragging my body after them down the sloping face of rock. My hands got a temporary grip where my feet had been on the ledge, but by then my legs were swinging wildly below the ledge, where the undercut rock-face gave them no hope of a foothold. I hung like that for a moment, trying instinctively to retain my grip on the wet rock of the ledge, but knowing all the time that I could never in any case pull myself back

177

onto it. Then my hands lost their grip, as my feet had, first one, then the other, and I began to fall.

So far as the fall went, I was lucky in two ways. For one, I fell feet first, and I was wearing my heavy boots, which gave my feet a lot of protection when I landed. For another, I fell at exactly the right moment, when a wave was rolling along the bottom of the face, so that I fell, not onto bare rock, but into a chest-high surge of moving water. But that was as far as my luck went. For the rest, I was in dire trouble at once. I felt my boots strike the rock under me, but there was no hope whatever of getting any sort of foothold. The water rolled me bodily along with it, as helpless as a piece of drift-wood in the grip of that enormous force, and the next moment I was washed clear of the rocks and had nothing but deep water under me. Whatever my boots had done for me when I fell, they were as much of an aid to swimming as the gangster's traditional bucket of cement. I went under at once and surfaced slowly. For a moment I got my head clear, choking and fighting for breath against the bitter salt water which had forced itself into my nose and mouth, and then the next wave rolled over me, and my head went under again. I fought madly in the grip of total fear and despair, but there was nothing constructive in my fighting, simply an instinctive struggle to keep my head above water long enough to get half a lungful of air before the sea pulled me under again. Seeing what happened, I know I must have made quite a fight of it, but there was only one way it could end.

What happened was that at some point in my agony that same pair of arms like boa-constrictors closed round my body under my threshing arms, and the same light voice spoke from behind my head. "Relax," it said. "Don't struggle, for Christ's sake. Lie back and let me take you. Cover your face if you can, or you'll bloody drown on the surface."

I had just enough conscious command of myself left to do what he said. I surrendered to the drag of those enormous arms and the thrust of enormous legs under me, and put one hand up, covering my mouth and nose against the intermittent surge of salt water over them. Presently the voice said, "Now. The rock's just behind you. I'll turn you to face it, and then climb, you bugger, climb." I felt myself spun round in the water, and then there was a sloping rock-face in front of me, and reached for it desperately with hands and feet, driven on by a single powerful thrust from behind. I was clear of the water at last, dragging my water-logged body up the wet slope of rock, when the voice behind me said, "Hold on, there's a wave coming," and for one last time the two of us crouched there, holding on more with Claudio's strength than with mine, while the water surged over us and rolled on, leaving us still clinging like outsize molluscs to the sea-scarred face of the rock. Then he said, "Climb," again, and a moment later I felt turf under me, not under my feet, but under my bruised and bleeding knees as I crawled, without dignity, but with unspeakable relief, finally out of the reach of that damned rolling sea.

For perhaps ten seconds I just stayed where I was, trying to collect my wits for what lay ahead. In a physical sense I was completely at Claudio's mercy. I myself knew that there was nothing left between us worth fighting for, but I faced the bleak fact that my survival depended on my ability to make him believe that. It is difficult at the best of times to prove that A is not B, even to an open-minded man. I had to prove it from a position of total physical inferiority to a man who had built his life for twenty years round the belief that A was B, and that one of these days he would be able to prove it. And I had no evidence of any sort. I could, if he would let me, take him up and show him the rock-fall and the monkey's head, but without Peter's letter they meant nothing, and I had destroyed Peter's letter a year ago precisely to prevent its falling into Claudio's hands.

The voice behind me said, "On your feet, soldier, and don't turn round. Just go where I say." I got up and went where he said. The fact that this big man with the soft West Country voice was borrowing his dialogue from a second-feature American movie was no comfort to me at all. Once when I hesitated I felt the short sharp dig in the small of my back that was almost a cliché in itself, and had not, in the state I was in, the wit to wonder how a man who had just emerged from the sea could have a workable gun in his hand. I think I knew from the start where we were going, but there was still nothing I could do about it. I was at the lower end of the ledge, barely six feet clear of the sea, and facing up it when he finally told me to stop. "All right," he said, "you can turn round now."

I turned, and there he was, a couple of yards away, facing me. "Good God," I said, "it's Charlie Tuke."

Charlie grinned at me but said nothing. His bullet head was hatless, his fair hair was gummed down on it with salt water, his moustache had lost its panache, but he still grinned at me. I said, "Thank you for pulling me out, Charlie. I doubt if it was pure benevolence, but thanks all the same." He still said nothing. He brought his right hand slowly and threateningly out of his jacket pocket, and then opened it suddenly to disclose a sharp-ended pebble. He threw the pebble into the sea and at once, with a movement so quick I could hardly follow it, put his hand into a niche in the rock beside him and brought it out holding a dry, clean and very real automatic.

He said almost apologetically, "I let yours go in the sea. Well, I mean, it wouldn't have been any good to you, not full of salt water like that. Not that I blame you for that. You didn't know you were going in the water. I did, and left mine behind." He thought for a moment. "My hat, too," he said. He reached into the same niche, this time with his left hand, and brought out the hat I had already seen once that day. He put it on, as Lisa had said, a little on one side, and seemed to feel the better for it. "All right," he said. "Up you go, Ben, my boy. There's no need to face the rock. You can do it just as well with your back to it. And it's your face I shall want to see, not your back. Up you go, then. I'll be right behind you."

I did as I was told. I was not consciously playing for time. I was simply letting things take their course until the crunch came. It was in fact easier going up the ledge leaning back against the rock face than it had been leaning forward. You could see so much better what you were doing. We did not go right up to the break, but we were a good twenty feet above the rocks and the breaking sea when he told me to stop. Enough to frighten me, I thought, especially when I had gone down once already.

"Now," he said, "I know you haven't got it on you. Where is it, then?"

This was it. I turned my head and looked direct into his big blue eyes, a couple of yards from mine, and because of the slope of the ledge, almost on a level. I said, "I know where it is, Charlie. I found the place just now, just before I saw you coming after me. But I couldn't get at it. The thing itself, I mean. Nor can you, nor can anyone else. There's been a rock-fall since Peter put it there, and it's got God knows how many tons of rock on top of it. There's nothing anyone can do about it."

181

Under his tilted hat his red forehead wrinkled in an effort to understand, but it was not a very willing effort. His heart was not in it. There was only one thing he wanted to understand, and I was saying something different. The big blue eyes looked at me, but I knew as I looked into them exactly what Lisa had meant. They were not quite looking at me, or at anything that was really there at all. They were looking at something Charlie saw in his own mind, whether it was there or not. He had stopped grinning now. I would not say his mouth was set hard, it was not that sort of mouth, but it had taken on an aggrieved, almost petulant look. If he had asked a question, or several questions, as he so well might have in view of what I had said, it would not have been so bad, but he did not. He said the one thing I did not want him to say. He said, "I don't believe you."

He said it quite calmly, as if it was the obvious and reasonable thing to say. He leant solidly back against the rock, with his heels on the ledge and the toes of his big brown shoes sticking out over it. He looked so comfortable, he could have eaten his dinner there. Only his right hand, on my side, was held firm against the rock with the gun pointing at me, not at my vitals, but at my legs about the level of the knee. A bullet in the knee, and down I'd go, still fully conscious and able to appreciate drowning when it happened. It was all very well calculated to break down my resistence, only I could not seem to persuade him that I was now no longer resisting.

I said, "Look, Charlie, do try to understand." I felt genuinely sorry for him in his inevitable disappointment, sorry but at the same time exasperated, as if I was trying to tell a grown child the truth about Father Christmas, or even about its own father. "Peter left me a letter telling me where he had put the thing. He'd buried it in the turf at the foot of a rock, and the top of the rock was shaped like a monkey's head. That was how I was to recognise it. Well, I've found the monkey's head. It's up there. But it's fallen, and most of the damned rock has come down with it. On top of the place where Peter buried the box, don't you see? I can show you—"

I made a move sideways along the ledge, but he said, "Stay where you are," and I stayed. He looked at me for a moment or two. There was no animosity in his look. I am prepared to swear that he thought I was being as unreasonable as I thought he was. "Look," he said. It was characteristic of the whole conversation that we kept telling each other to look. "Look," he said, "let's be clear on one thing. If I don't get it, you're not going to. Either you tell me where it is, or you go back in the sea, and this time I won't pull you out. And the sea's not one of your favourite things, Ben, is it? Never was, as I remember. Now, come on. I'll give you a minute or two, but no more."

We must have heard the sound simultaneously, because we both, regardless of each other, turned our heads back over our shoulders and looked up towards the top of the rock face. I myself saw nothing, and I do not think Charlie did either, because he leant the whole top of his body foward, craning his neck round for a better view. That was what did for him, poor Charlie. The stone must have weighed all of ten pounds, and it caught him, not on his gun arm, which was what it was probably aimed at, but behind his right shoulder. The whole upper part of his body jerked forward, and then his weight was outside his feet. For what seemed seconds he stood there on the ledge, bent right forward from the hips, flailing his arms round and round as if he was trying to fly back to the vertical. It is a thing you see clowns and slapstick comedians do before falling headfirst into the

183

water-tank or the outsize custard pie. Like that, it can look very comic, but done in earnest it is grotesque and horrible. In either case, the end is the same. The whole of his body was below them before his big feet left the ledge, and, unlike me earlier, he fell headfirst onto bare rock.

He fell well out, and for a moment or two I had a perfectly clear view of him. He lay on his back, spread-eagled on the rock. His hat had fallen off, and even as I looked at him the red drained out of the big upturned face and was replaced by a spreading red stain on the wet rock under him. His eyes were wide open, but he did not move. Then the sea rolled over him, and when it was gone, he was gone, too.

I started sideways down the ledge. I had only one idea in mind, and it was Lisa's voice that stopped me. If she had called me by name or begged me not to go, I do not think I should have taken any notice, but she did neither. She said very clearly and incisively, "Don't be a fool." That stopped me. Then she said again, "Don't be a fool, Ben. He was probably dead before he went in the water. If he wasn't, he probably is by now. You couldn't get him out alive. You couldn't get him out at all. You probably couldn't get yourself out if you went in. Let him go, Ben. It's all for the best."

I stayed where I was, staring down at the rolling water below me. I could not see Claudio anywhere. Then, in a patch of clear water, I saw his hat. It floated on the sea the right way up, and even there, it seemed to me, a little on one side. Perhaps it had just got into the way of it. Then the sea rolled over it and the hat too was gone. I stared for a moment longer, and then began working my way back down the slope of the ledge.

I showed Lisa the rock-fall and monkey's head, just to make my point, but we did not find much to say to each other. She knew better than to say again that it was all for the best. I could see that for myself. Claudio had fallen fully dressed into the sea, knocking his head in the process, and if his body came ashore, there would be no awkward questions to answer. Just another fool visitor asking for it. It happened every year. It was the perfect solution, but that did not make me like it any better. And I was cold in my wet clothes.

Later, when I had driven Lisa back to her grey Minor, and seen her set off for the town, I turned the Triumph back onto the coast-road and drove south-westwards to the corner of the island. I was warm enough in the car with the heater on, and I did not want to go back yet. There was the light-house itself, which I had seen before only as a flashing light, standing up tall and slender on its outlying reef, with the swell bursting sullenly over the half-exposed rocks round it. I pulled the car to the side of the road and sat there, with my eyes on the moving sea and the unmoving column of stone and my mind on Claudio.

I found it easier, still, to think of him as Claudio, not as the long forgotten and briefly rediscovered Charlie Tuke. It was with Claudio I was concerned, not with Charlie, and I wondered why I felt about him as I did. I thought no one is a hero to himself except the Claudios among us, and the Claudios do fearful things on the strength of their convic-tion, and some of them get away with it and some do not. My Claudio was a crackpot, but I could not see that he was any more contemptible a character than the one in the play. My Claudio had stabbed my best friend in the back by mis-take and ruined Lisa's life doing it, and the Claudio in the play had ruined the girl he was supposed to be in love with to satisfy his own male vanity. But the one in the play had finished up with the girl and the money, and my Claudio had finished up with a broken head in a breaking sea, and I could not think that this was really fair. He had been braver and stronger than I, and even, crackpot as he was, a little cleverer, and I had lost nothing in the encounter except the last illusions of my own heroism. I had done fearful things in my time myself, but I was not the man for them now. Benedick, in the end, had not killed his Claudio for all Beatrice's saying, and I had not killed mine for all Lisa's. But I knew of one Claudio, at least, whom we had killed between the lot of us, and he was better dead. I thought you could do worse things, after all, than being a night-watchman. You could no doubt do better things, too, but I did not think being an estate-agent in Brancastle was one of them.

But my drying clothes were sticking to me, full of salt and sand from that churned-up water, and I could not sort the thing out now. I pulled the car onto the road again and set off for the town.

>>> If you've enjoyed this book and would like to discover more great vintage crime and thriller titles, as well as the most exciting crime and thriller authors writing today, visit: >>>

The Murder Room
Where Criminal Minds Meet

themurderroom.com